"Nice to meet yo[u"]

Mia let Nate take her h[and] she felt an unexpected [   ]

"Nice to meet you, too," she replied as his smile deepened.

"So you own the flower store," he said, dropping his cowboy hat back on his head. "That's ambitious," he continued.

"It definitely keeps me busy."

For this brief moment, Mia didn't feel like a mommy weighed down with obligations. She returned his smile.

Just then her friend Sophie arrived, pushing the buggy, wails emanating from it. "I think one of your little girls is hungry," she said to Mia.

Mia caught Nate frowning at her.

"Those are your kids?" he asked. "Sorry, I didn't know you were—"

"A mom?" Mia couldn't stop the hint of annoyance entering her voice. "It gets worse. There's two more of these at home," she said.

Nate wasn't the first man put off by her brood.

He was, however, the first man she'd felt any attraction to in a long, long time.

Books by Carolyne Aarsen

Love Inspired

CAROLYNE AARSEN

and her husband, Richard, live on a small ranch in northern Alberta, where they have raised four children and numerous foster children, and are still raising cattle. Carolyne crafts her stories in an office with a large west-facing window, through which she can watch the changing seasons while struggling to make her words obey.

A Father in the Making

Carolyne Aarsen

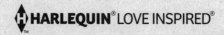

Recycling programs
for this product may
not exist in your area.

™ LOVE INSPIRED BOOKS

ISBN-13: 978-0-373-87878-9

A FATHER IN THE MAKING

Copyright © 2014 by Carolyne Aarsen

www.Harlequin.com

Printed in U.S.A.

Forget the former things; do not dwell on the past.

—*Isaiah* 43:18

For Lorna Strydhorst, faithful reader and friend.

Chapter One

"Go to sleep. Please go back to sleep," Mia pleaded as she dragged the stroller holding her twin toddlers backward into the bookstore. Jennifer had been fussing for the past twenty minutes. She couldn't be hungry. Mia had given both baby girls and her two sons a good supper before heading out the door into the cool of the late-fall evening. A better supper than she managed to wolf down before her babysitter, Angie, showed up. Though Angie wasn't her regular babysitter, she had offered to take the two boys and the twins. Mia took care of four children all the time, but she didn't feel right doing that to a temporary babysitter so she had taken the twins with her.

Fatigue dragged at her, and for a moment Mia entertained the idea of skipping the bookstore. However, she had promised Josh and Nico she would get the books. And ever since her husband had left her pregnant with twins and two preschool sons, Mia was firm on keeping promises to Josh and Nico.

As Jennifer's whimpers turned into a cry of protest, Mia fished a pacifier out of the overstuffed diaper bag dangling from the handles of the stroller. She wiped the lint off and eased the pacifier into Jennifer's mouth. Her daughter resisted a moment and then the pacifier began bouncing as the baby eagerly sucked on it.

Really? Shouldn't one-year-olds be weaned off pacifiers by now?

Mia closed off the scolding voice in her head—Other Mother, the annoying amalgamation of every parenting article she had ever read, with a pinch of her perfect sister thrown in.

"Hey, my dear girl, shall I take the twins around the store while you shop?"

Sophie Brouwer smiled at Mia over the top of the stroller, her bright blue eyes surrounded by a network of friendly wrinkles. She wore her usual velour jogging suit today in a shade of bubblegum-pink that no female over ten should wear. And Sophie was easily six decades past that.

"I'll be okay," was Mia's automatic reply.

Sophie shook her head and nudged Mia aside. "Don't be so independent." Sophie grasped the handles of the stroller. "You go talk to your friend."

Then she pushed the stroller behind a shelf of books, leaving Mia no choice but to go to Evangeline.

Her friend was crouched down on the floor behind the counter, her long skirt puddling around her as she sorted through a box of books. Evangeline straightened as she saw Mia and pushed her long hair back from her face with a smile. "Hey, girl. Where're the kids?"

"Angie is taking care of the boys and Sophie just kidnapped the twins."

"You want a cup of coffee before I get your books?" Evangeline asked, waving a delicate hand toward the back of the store, her diamond engagement ring refracting the overhead light.

Mia's mouth watered, and for a moment she allowed a "maybe" to test her resolve.

"Only if it's quick," she said, keeping her voice firm as if to convince herself as much as her friend. "I have to catch Mr. Truscott before he closes up his law office for the night."

"What about?"

Mia sighed. "The usual. Support payments from Al, who's disappeared off the radar again. And after that I have to get groceries and pick up my van from the mechanic." She fought down the usual panic that hovered over her every day. Too much to do and not enough time to get it all done. "Hey, have you heard from Renee and Zach today? My phone's been wonky."

"I got a note from Renee this morning. I can't believe she's texting us on her honeymoon," Evangeline said as she walked to the room in the back that doubled as a storage room and meeting place for the book club that Evangeline hosted every other week. "And why is Angie babysitting for you? What happened to Blythe, your usual babysitter?"

"Blythe had some hot date tonight. Lucky her." Mia leaned against the doorway as Evangeline sorted through the books she had ordered for other customers.

"Hey, someday your prince will come," Evangeline said.

"I can't afford to let a prince into my children's lives and I have no energy or time for romance. This morning I was so tired I punched my passcode for my bank account into my microwave."

Evangeline gave her a sympathetic look as the jangling of the bell above the entrance announced more customers.

Then Mia heard the murmur of male voices in the store behind them. "I think Denny's here," Evangeline said, looking past Mia with such pleasure Mia couldn't stop a faint twinge of envy.

They walked out of the room just as Sophie Brouwer walked past them, pushing the stroller toward the two men standing by the till. One Mia recognized as Denny, Evangeline's fiancé. The other man was unfamiliar. He wore a cowboy hat like Denny, but his had a feather in the band. His twill shirt was torn at the elbow and accompanied by worn blue jeans and scuffed cowboy boots. As Sophie passed them, the unfamiliar man crouched down, reached out and took Jennifer's finger.

"Hey, you two cuties," Mia heard him say with a laugh as Jennifer gurgled and Grace, awake now, batted at his cowboy hat. "Easy on the hat," he said, letting Grace grab his other hand. "It's been through enough."

Denny grinned at the girls, but walked around the stroller to Evangeline and gave her a quick kiss.

"Looks like Nate is in love again," he said with a laugh as he looked from Mia to the man playing with her twins.

The man Mia assumed was Nate stood, still grinning down at the girls. His brown hair spilled across his broad forehead from beneath the brim of his cowboy hat, giving him a casual look. His hazel eyes had a fan of wrinkles at the corners. The eyes of a man who worked outside, squinting against the sun. His hands were tucked in the pockets of his jeans, his thumbs resting on a wide buckle that Mia assumed had, at one time, been a prize in a rodeo. His rolled-up shirtsleeves revealed muscular forearms.

An appealing package, she thought, unconsciously tucking a stray strand of short hair behind her ear.

"They're cute as buttons," Nate said, glancing from the girls back to Mia as Sophie pushed the stroller away, obviously happy to keep watching them. Mia had to get going, too, but she found herself unwilling to leave. Especially with this attractive man giving her a steady look and a flirty smile.

"Evangeline, look who came rolling into town this morning. My little brother, Nate." Denny laid a hand on the handsome man's shoulder, solving the temporary mystery. Mia had heard bits and pieces about Nate, Denny's foster brother. She knew he trained and rode cutting horses in competitions. A loner who worked at various ranches over the winter and was on the road all summer following the cutting horse circuit. Charming, attractive, single and unsuitable.

Not that Mia was looking.

Nate pulled his hat off, messing up his thick, brown hair and reached out to shake Evangeline's hand.

"Poor guy had a wreck with his horses this morning and he needs a place to hole up for a while and for his horses to heal," Denny continued. "I told him he could stay with me. On the ranch."

"I'm so sorry to hear that," Evangeline said, turning to Nate, concern in her voice. "Are the horses okay? How did it happen?"

Nate's gaze drifted from Mia to Evangeline. "I got cut off by a semi and had to hit the ditch. My horse trailer rolled. Tango is banged up pretty bad. Thankfully, my mare, Nola, is okay as are the other two mares. Dog was shook up a bit, but he's okay."

"Oh, my goodness, what a fright," Evangeline said. "Of course you can stay on the ranch. Olivia is taking care of Ella right now, and she's staying in the trailer, but she's leaving tonight so you can stay there."

"I don't want to push anyone out," Nate protested, his eyes cutting back to Mia's again. "And if Socks is a problem I'm sure—"

"You and your dog are more than welcome."

"But you and Denny are getting married—"

"In half a year. I still live above this store until that happy event." Then she glanced over at Mia and lifted a hand in apology. "Sorry. I'm forgetting my manners. Nate, this is my friend Mia VerBeek. She runs the flower shop next door."

Nate turned his full attention back to Mia, his smile deepening.

"Nice to meet you, Mia," he said, his voice holding a hint of humor as he held his hand out.

You need to get going. You don't have time for this.

But Mia ignored Other Mother's chiding voice and let Nate take her hand. He held it a beat longer than necessary in his warm, rough one and when he let go, she felt an unexpected moment of loss.

"Nice to meet you, too," she replied as his smile widened, creating a curl of attraction.

"So you own the flower store," he said, dropping his hat back on his head and slipping his hands into the back pockets of his worn jeans. Was it her overactive imagination or was he leaning closer? "That's ambitious," he continued.

Desperate, actually. Mia needed to support her family after Al ditched and then divorced her. She had no marketable skills. Candace, the previous owner, cut her a good deal on a ten-year buyout and had spent time training her. It wasn't Mia's dream job, but it was work and it came with an apartment above the store. The whole setup had been an answer to many desperate prayers Mia had sent toward God.

"It definitely keeps me busy." Mia held his gaze a beat longer than she knew she should. His smile grew and when he shifted his weight it moved him a few inches closer.

Walk away now, Mia. This man is flirting with you and we both know how that will end.

Mia knew she should listen to Other Mother's prim advice, but for this small moment she felt like an attractive and desirable woman. She didn't feel like Professional Mommy weighed down with obligations. Of course she loved her children, but still...

She returned his smile.

Just then Sophie arrived, pushing the stroller, wails emanating from it. "I think one of your little girls is hungry," she said to Mia. "The one with the green bow in her hair."

"That would be Grace and she's probably thirsty." Mia shifted mental gears so quickly she was surprised she didn't hear a grinding sound. She turned the stroller to look inside at one very upset baby waving her chubby hands in protest, releasing another howl when she saw Mia. "Oh, honey," Mia murmured, lifting the wailing little girl out of the stroller, patting her on the behind. "What's wrong with you, munchkin? You thirsty?"

"You can heat up the bottle in the microwave in the

book club room if you need to feed her," Evangeline offered.

As Mia reached into the diaper bag to get a bottle she caught Nate frowning at her.

"Those are your kids?" he asked.

She didn't imagine the shuttering of his expression. Nor the step he took away from them. Like a rejection of her girls. Like Al.

"Sorry," he said. "I didn't know you were—"

"A mom?" Mia couldn't stop the hint of annoyance entering her voice. "It gets worse. There's two more of these at home and no father," she said, reality extinguishing the small attraction she had allowed herself to feel. Nate wasn't the first man put off by her brood.

She bounced Grace in her arms then turned back to Evangeline. "I'll heat up her milk and feed her. Thanks for the books. I'll pay for them on my way out."

"You know you don't have to—"

"I'll pay for them on my way out," she insisted, unable to stop herself from shooting a quick glance at Nate. He was still looking at her but the pity on his face ignited a flare of annoyance.

She juggled her baby in one hand and with the other worked the stroller around the desk. It caught on the corner and the diaper bag fell off, spilling diapers, bottles, snack packages, extra clothes and old cookies all over the floor.

Of course this would happen as she was trying to make a quick getaway. Of course this would happen in front of this handsome, single guy.

"Here. Let me help you." Nate stepped toward her and bent over to straighten the mess just as she reached for the bag. His hand brushed hers and to her dismay she felt a faint tingle again.

"I'm okay. I got this," she returned as Grace's wails grew in intensity.

But Nate set her and the large diaper bag on end.

"I'll take care of Jennifer." Sophie Brouwer made a sudden appearance and before Mia could say anything she wheeled the stroller and its lone passenger away. Evangeline showed up with a broom and nudged Mia aside. "I can finish this," she said.

"You should take care of your little girl," Nate said, glancing over at her as he gathered up the embarrassing detritus of her diaper bag.

"I'm sure I know what I need to do," she returned, frustration and pressure and everything that had piled on her shoulders the past few months making her snappier than normal.

She stood and strode to the back room with the sobbing baby. But by the time she got there she realized she had left the bottle of milk lying on the floor. With a groan of frustration she turned to get it, only to end up face-to-face with Nate in the doorway, holding out a bottle.

With a muttered thanks she took it from him, closed the door to the back room and rocked a now furious Gracie.

As soon as the milk was ready she snatched it out of the microwave and Gracie grabbed for it and shoved it in her mouth. Silence, blessed silence, now reigned and Mia dropped into the nearest chair, cuddled her little girl close and fought the inexplicable urge to break into tears.

* * *

Nate stood a moment by the door, listening. Guess Mia got her little girl settled.

"I feel like I have to apologize for Mia's shortness," Evangeline said as she stood. "She's a great girl. She's just had a lot to deal with lately."

"I imagine taking care of four kids would do that." He shot a quick glance over to where Sophie was pushing the stroller around and he couldn't help a smile at the sight of the little girl still sleeping inside it, her head fallen to one side, her cute mouth open.

"Mia's had a tough go of it," Evangeline agreed as she set the diaper bag on the counter.

"Doesn't help that she's so independent," Denny said, still leaning an elbow on the counter.

"She's had to be," Evangeline retorted, as if sticking up for her friend.

Nate could identify. He had come limping, literally, with his broken-down horse trailer and injured horses and Socks, his dog, onto Denny's yard this morning feeling sheepish and reluctant. When he had his accident he had been on his way to deliver his mares to a ranch in Montana where he would be working after the competition he had entered Tango in. The vet in Cranbrook had told Nate that Tango wouldn't be competing anytime soon, and Nola might end up foaling earlier because of the accident. Thankfully, Bella was okay.

After being out of touch so long, Nate felt like the prodigal son when he pulled onto Denny's yard.

But Denny had come running out and had pulled him close in a bear hug. Behind him had come his foster sister, Olivia, carrying a little girl. Denny's daughter, Nate found out later. Both Olivia, Nate's foster sister, and Ella were crying. Olivia from joy, Ella from frustration.

And as he stood with Denny's arm around his shoulder and Olivia's around his waist, Nate felt like he had come home.

"So, Nate, what do you think of my future wife's store?" Denny was asking, leaning on the counter as he flipped through the children's books Mia had left behind.

As Nate glanced around the building with its high ceilings, wooden floor and bookshelves lining every wall, he felt a craving rise up in him.

"This old store is cool," he said with a grin. "And all those shelves of new books just waiting to be cracked open."

"So you like to read?" she asked.

"*Like* to read?" Denny snorted. "This cowboy had his nose in a book so often I can't believe he's not short-sighted. Used to read on the way to school, on the way back, when he was riding fence. I had to snap my fingers in his face to get him to look up and even then he would barely notice me. You probably have at least three books with you now."

Nate just grinned. "There are two in my truck and a few more in my backpack."

Denny shook his head. "Of course there are."

The other baby girl in the stroller the older lady was pushing around let out a squawk, which made him wonder how Mia was making out with the little girl. And then he wondered why he cared. Someone like her was so out of his comfort zone, she may as well be in another country. It would be difficult enough for him to bring another person into his life, let alone another person with four kids. Then the back door of the store opened up and Mia came out, and in spite of his self-talk he couldn't stop himself from taking another look.

She was petite. Cute. Her dark hair cut in a short, pixie-looking cut. Her brown eyes were like a doe's, large, brown, thick-lashed and held a hint of sadness. This, in turn, created a protective urge that surprised him.

He pushed down the reaction. He was in no position to protect anyone. He was having a hard enough time taking care of himself.

"Everything okay?" Evangeline asked as Mia walked over to where the older lady named Sophie stood, reading a book with one hand, pushing the stroller back and forth with another.

"Yeah. She's settled. Hopefully that lasts until I get back to the store."

"Hey, Mia," Denny said. "Nate and I came to take Evangeline out for supper. You want to join us?"

"Sorry," Mia said with a smile of regret. "I have to catch Zach's father before he quits for the night and I've got a ton of other things to do yet."

She didn't look at Nate this time and he was confident he was part of the reason she turned down the invitation. He felt like he should apologize for his reaction but then caught himself. Apologizing was Denny's thing.

He was always the one who felt like he had to smooth things over with Olivia, Adrianna and Trista. Nate would hunker down, avoid eye contact and keep himself from getting caught in the emotional storms. They usually blew over quickly in the Norquest family.

As for Mia, Nate knew he wouldn't be spending

much time with her. As soon as Tango was healed, he would be on the road again. Back to a life that he was more comfortable with.

Just him and his horses and no one depending on him.

Chapter Two

Was that smoke she smelled?

Mia took another sniff as she walked out of the grocery store, the evening light slanting over the parking lot. Probably just her overactive imagination.

As she came around the corner of Mug Shots, she heard Evangeline call her name. She was leaving the café, Denny and Nate right behind her.

"You only now finished your grocery shopping?" Evangeline asked.

"Talking to Zach took longer than I thought, and the grocery store was busy today." As they walked along the street, she tried to ignore Nate's presence behind them. She didn't need to mix up her life by getting distracted by someone like him.

"Is that smoke I smell?" Nate asked.

"Yeah. I thought I smelled it, too." Then she looked up and saw a plume of black smoke in the sky above Mug Shots. Her heart stopped.

"Looks like it's coming from Main Street," she said as she hurried her steps, trying to shake off the idea that it could be her store and home. Then she took another look and saw smoke twining around the telltale crooked brick chimney of her store. Panic clenched her stomach as she grabbed the handles of her stroller and hurried down the street.

"Mia. Wait," Denny called out, but she ignored him, her panic growing with each step. And then she came around the corner.

"It's my store." Her legs turned to rubber as she clung to the handles of the stroller. "My boys. My boys." She started across the street, unable to move fast enough.

Someone caught her by the arm. She shook it off, her entire focus on the smoke pouring out of her store and flames starting to curl up from the roof. She started walking again, but then an arm snaked around her waist. "Don't. Stay here," Nate's voice growled in her ear as his iron-hard arm clamped her against him. "You can't do anything."

"My boys. My boys are in there." She thrashed against his hands, her fear and panic twisting like the flames now flickering from the roof. "My boys and Angie."

She heard the squawk of a two-way radio and then heard another voice behind her.

She spun around. Jeff Deptuck, a local fireman, stood beside her, his cell phone to his ear and a two-way radio in his other hand. She grabbed at him. "Jeff. They're not here yet. My boys are in there with Angie."

"Are you sure?" Jeff's gaze was suddenly intent on hers. "Angie and your boys?"

"Look, someone is at the window," Nate called out. It was Angie, waving. She was probably trapped.

"The trucks are out of town. They won't be here for

another ten minutes," Jeff called out. "Someone get an extension ladder from the hardware store."

A tall man broke away from the group that had gathered and ran down the street.

"By the time he gets the ladder out, it's going to be too late," Mia called out.

"We'll have to go in up the stairs at the back," Jeff said.

"I'm coming with you," Nate said. "I've worked as a volunteer firefighter."

"You listen to me and do exactly what I say," Jeff warned, his voice stern.

Then without another word, Jeff dashed across the street then ducked into the gap between the buildings to get to the alley, Nate right behind him.

"Make sure she doesn't go anywhere," Nate said to Denny, then ran across the street after Jeff.

Mia pulled at Denny's hands that held her arms like a vise. "I need to go and help them," she called out. "I know how to get in."

But Denny pulled Mia back again as the ominous sound of fire crackling battled with the growing wail of sirens.

But it was only a police car that came down Main Street.

"The fire trucks aren't coming," Mia sobbed, pulling ineffectually at Denny's hands. She stared up at Angie's panicked figure in the window. "They won't get here in time."

Then Angie disappeared and Mia's heart turned to ice.

She couldn't watch, but she couldn't look away,

thoughts, fears and half-formed images seething and twisting through her tortured mind.

The policemen got out and moved the gathering crowd back.

Mia's entire attention was on the building and the smoke billowing out of it now. After what seemed to be hours, the fire trucks finally showed up at the end of the street, the men piling out in a flurry of activity, their bulky suits and reflective tape flashing in the failing sunlight.

"Stay here, Mia. Evangeline, you make her stay," Denny warned as he ran toward the firefighters calling out that there were people in the building yet. One of the firefighters spoke with him while others donned masks and hooked tanks over their bulky coats. There were still more who worked in a rhythm, laying out the hoses, hooking them to the nearest fire hydrant. Instructions were called out, verified as the men with masks grabbed their axes and entered the front of the store.

Then, with a whistle of steam, water was poured onto the building and into the open window. Then more sirens as ambulances came, blue-and-red lights strobing through the smoke and gathering dusk.

Neither Evangeline nor Denny spoke as the drama unfolded in front of them, but Mia felt their hands on her, holding her back, yet at the same time, comforting her.

"Dear Lord, please keep Jeff and Nate safe. Help them to get Angie, Nico and Josh out of the store," she heard Evangeline praying aloud.

Mia couldn't pray, her gaze stuck on the building. The brick facade was now charred with smoke and dripping with water as the flames momentarily retreated.

Where were the boys? Jeff? Nate? Time ceased as her world narrowed down to the building with smoke pouring out of the windows, the shouts of the firemen, the drone of water pumps, the hiss of flames being extinguished and the cries of the onlookers now gathered along the street.

Then another wave of noise caught her attention. It came from a side avenue. People shouting. Cheering.

Then she saw them.

Jeff, limping as he carried Josh, supported by Angie.

And behind him, Nate holding Nico close, his head tucked against his neck.

Mia ran toward them, her heart threatening to burst in her chest.

"Josh. Nico." She reached out her arms to take them. But just as she got close, EMT personnel came between her and her boys, taking them from Jeff and Nate and escorting Angie to the ambulance.

"Those are my boys," she called out, desperate to find out how they were.

"They're okay." Nate came up beside her, reeking of smoke, his face smeared with soot. She caught at him, her fingers digging into his arm.

"Are you sure? Are you sure?"

Nate looked down at her, then gave her a tentative smile. "We managed to get them out before the fire got too intense."

Her legs gave out as the reaction sank in. Nate caught her before she fell. "C'mon, let's go see how your boys are," he said, slipping his arm around her shoulder and holding her up. Together they walked to the ambulance, him supporting her, her entire attention focused like a laser on the back of the ambulance.

Yet, at the same time, she was filled with gratitude for the man holding her up. The man who had rescued her sons.

"Are you sure you're okay?" Denny held Nate's gaze with an intensity Nate tried to ignore. It only reminded him of how close he and Jeff had cut things getting Angie, Nico and Josh out of the building.

"The paramedic said I'm fine, so I'll take his word for that." Nate leaned forward in the hard plastic chair of the hospital waiting room, and subconsciously tapped his foot on the shining surface floor. The sharp, anti-septic smell of the hospital brought back memories he thought he'd buried. Spent too much time here as a kid.

"You should never have run into that building, you know," Denny said.

"I had training," Nate protested, fighting the urge to get up and pace. "That other guy, Jeff, he couldn't get two kids and that woman out on his own. If we had waited till the fire department showed up, it might have been too late."

He didn't want to let his mind go too far down that road. In spite of his work as a volunteer fireman, he knew he would be reliving that harrowing search for months to come. The heat of the floor in Mia's apart-ment. The horror that gripped him when he made it to the bed and didn't find the little boy in it as Angie had said. His panicked sweep of the room only to find the little boy huddled in a closet, his arms wrapped around his knees.

Denny sat back in his chair and gave him a smile. "You're quite something, little brother. But you should let the doctor check you over."

"I'm fine. I just want to make sure that kid, Nico, is okay." The boy had scared him. When Nate pulled him out of the closet, he'd gone limp and Nate had to drag him out of the room and back down the stairs.

"Is Evangeline okay with taking care of those baby girls?" He wanted to talk about something else.

"Yeah. She's used to handling babies after little Ella came into our lives a couple of months ago."

"Hey, I was sorry to hear about your ex-wife's death," Nate said, a note of sympathy in his voice.

"It took some adjusting. Especially since Lila's sister dropped that bomb the same time she dropped Ella off on my doorstep because she didn't want to take care of her anymore."

"I still can't believe I've got a two-year-old niece," Nate said, letting a smile curve his lips. "And you're getting married again in a couple of months."

"I can't believe it, either, but I have to say, I highly recommend it."

Nate just snorted. "Being single is better for a guy like me. Less chance to get hurt." He stopped himself there. Denny always made him say more than he wanted.

He remembered coming to the Norquest ranch a young, angry boy of twelve, abused by his stepfather. Denny's family worked his way past the defenses Nate had spent the first twelve years of his life erecting.

The Norquests surrounded him with love and laughter and gave him a vision of a life that was good. Olivia, Trista and Adrianna teased him the same way they teased Denny. Steve and Donna Norquest treated him like their own. After two years of living with them he started calling them Mom and Dad.

Then, when Denny was seventeen, they died in a small plane crash, reinforcing the one belief he had clung to since his mother left him with an abusive stepfather.

Letting people into your life hurt.

"You'll change your mind someday," Denny said with a conviction that created a tinge of frustration in Nate.

But Nate preferred to keep his comments to himself.

Evangeline came toward them pushing the baby stroller and gave them both a quick smile. "I'll keep moving," she whispered as she passed them. "The girls are sleeping. I just called Olivia and she said she would stay until we came back."

Denny nodded and leaned back, seemingly content to just sit.

Nate envied him his composure. He couldn't sit still. Too much had happened too quickly. He was still processing his accident and now this?

He tapped his fingers together and blew out his breath, feeling as if the walls closed in on him.

"What is taking so long?"

"You can go back to the ranch if you want," Denny said. "Check on your horses. See how Olivia is doing."

Nate shook his head. "No. I want to see this through. Do you want something to drink? I'm dry as dust."

"No, thanks, but you go ahead. Do you need change?" he asked, already reaching for his wallet.

"Thanks. I'm good." Nate had to smile at the offer. Denny was always slipping him money when Nate blew through his allowance sooner than he was supposed to. Always looking out for him. Still looking out for him.

Nate walked down the hall to the vending machine

and made his choice, but when he pulled his wallet out to slip the money in he was disappointed to see his fingers trembling.

Aftershock, he reminded himself. The paramedic told him to watch out for it and to go to the hospital if it got too bad.

As if. He had spent enough of his life in a hospital; he wasn't going to deliberately check into one on his own. He grabbed the bottle of juice when it dropped into the bin. He twisted the top off and chugged half the bottle down as his mind, unwilling, returned to the thick, choking smoke curling up from the building. The panic that seized him when he saw the flames licking up the side of the wall as he and Jeff pulled open the door to the apartment, dropped to the floor and started crawling. The fear that clutched at him when he didn't find the little boy in his bed.

He stopped by the windows overlooking the town as he walked back to the waiting room, pushing the memories down. Hartley Creek seemed like a good place to stay awhile if he had to stay anywhere. Denny was here. Olivia, too. And it sounded like the other sisters might be popping in from time to time.

Nate let a hint of a smile play over his lips. He had missed Denny and the girls more than he wanted to admit. The past three years had been tiring and taxing and draining. Too much time on the road. Too many competitions. Too much juggling to find places for his horses to stay on the off-season. Right now he had two mares that had just foaled, boarded at a friend's place. One of these days he knew he had to find a permanent home.

But the thought of settling down, putting down roots, creating the potential for loss...

He shook off that thought, took another swig of juice and started back down the hallway. Then stopped as another fit of coughing seized him. Unable to walk through it he rested his hand against the wall, doubled over. When he was done, his chest felt as if someone had doused his lungs with acid. He took a few more slow breaths, carefully sucking air into his raw throat. It would be okay, he reminded himself.

Then, as he looked up, he saw Mia standing by the entrance to the emergency department, her arms wrapped tightly around her oldest boy. She was looking directly at him.

For a moment he felt it again. The initial shot of attraction he had experienced when he first saw her in Evangeline's bookstore. The attraction that had been doused when he found out that she had children. A family.

But in spite of that, he easily remembered how she leaned into him as they walked toward the ambulance. How, for a moment, it felt nice to be needed.

He pushed that reaction down. He had his own stuff to deal with and no room for a woman in his life. Especially not a woman who needed more than he could possibly give.

"Where are Evangeline and Denny?" he asked her as he came around the corner to see the waiting room vacated.

"The girls just woke up when I got back here. One needed something to eat, the other, a clean diaper. So they're taking care of it."

He sensed, from the strained note in her voice that

she didn't feel right about that situation. She seemed like a person that had a hard time accepting help.

"So how are the boys?" he asked. "What did the doctor say?"

She took a breath then pushed her hand through her short hair in a nervous gesture. "Josh is good," she said, rubbing her hand up and down the arm of the older boy standing beside her. His dark hair was pasted down on one side and while his face was clean, his hands were still streaked with black, as were his clothes. Mia fingered Josh's hair away from his face in a vain attempt to neaten it, her fingers trembling. "You're going to need a bath when we get home, buddy...." Mia's sentence trailed off and Nate realized she no longer had a home to go back to.

"How is Nico?" Nate asked.

Mia gave him a curious look, as if wondering about his concern. "Dr. Brouwer is checking a few more things out. How was he when you took him out of the building?"

"Scared. Panicky. He hung on to me like a little monkey. But I don't think anything was broken or burned."

Mia pressed her lips together as she took a slow, trembling breath. "I can't begin to thank you for...for what you did. You saved my son's life."

She gave him a wavery smile and Nate had to resist the urge to slip his arm around her shoulder and support her. But he caught himself in time.

He had nothing to give a woman like her. She needed someone stable, strong. Someone who could be a father to her kids.

Instead, he turned to Josh, feeling a rush of empathy. Hospitals could be intimidating and scary places.

Nate crouched down, balancing on the balls of his feet, his hands dangling between his knees. "Hey. How are you feeling?"

Josh gave him a smile that echoed his mother's. Trying to be brave. "I was scared in the fire," the six-year-old said. "And then I saw Mr. Deptuck and he got me and Angie out." His lower lip trembled and Nate guessed he would have a few bad dreams the next while.

Nate put his hand on his shoulder and squeezed lightly. "You'll be just fine, champ."

He straightened and caught Mia's gaze, her eyes holding a stark look, a direct contrast to the forced smile that held her mouth captive.

She was trying so hard to be brave, he thought. Brave for her son.

"And Jeff?" he asked.

"I'm not sure." She shot him a frown. "Are you sure you shouldn't see the doctor, as well?"

The concern in her voice created a flicker of warmth, but he waved off her suggestion. "I'm fine. Throat's sore, but I'm okay."

She looked at him like she didn't believe him and for a moment, he found he couldn't look away.

Stop this, he warned himself. *Don't do this.*

Then he heard the sound of a baby's whimper and he spun around. Denny and Evangeline returned with the girls. Both babies rubbed their eyes, their cheeks flaming pink.

"Oh, girlies," Mia said, reaching out for one of them. "You are exhausted."

Evangeline released the one baby to her and Mia held her close, tucking her little baby's head against her neck and rocking her. She had been through a lot and was still giving her babies comfort.

A loving mother.

"So we need to figure out what to do with you and the kids," Evangeline said, her voice taking on a brisk, no-nonsense tone. "Denny and I think you should come back to the ranch with us."

"I can leave if you need the space," Nate said.

"No. Your horse is in no shape to travel," Denny replied. "We got it figured. Evangeline can't go back to her apartment above the store until things are cleaned up so Mia, Evangeline and the kids can move into the house with Olivia. Me and you get the trailer," he said to Nate.

Nate wanted to protest, but knew he wasn't in any position to. His horses needed to recuperate and he needed to be close to them. The foals the mares carried were part of his stake for a new venture he hoped to set up someday. When he was ready to settle.

"So, Mia, it's decided," Denny said with what sounded to Nate like a forced heartiness.

"I don't know," Mia said, glancing over her shoulder to the examining rooms. "I don't want to put you out. I could stay with my mother and father."

Seemed like she didn't want to stay on the ranch any more than he did, Nate thought.

"Your parents live in a minuscule apartment in Nelson," Evangeline said. "You can't go there with four kids."

Mia sighed and closed her eyes as if she still wasn't sure what to do.

"Just come for the next couple of nights," Evangeline said, slipping her arm around her friend's shoulders. "Don't think too far ahead."

Mia nodded and released a sigh. Denny rocked the other baby watching both of them with a fatherly look.

Nate stood on the edge of the group feeling like the outsider he was.

Then the curtain dividing the waiting area from the emergency department swished aside and the doctor stood in the entrance, motioning for Mia to come.

And he wasn't smiling.

Chapter Three

"So you're saying he can't talk because of the trauma he experienced?" Mia rubbed her index finger over her chin in a nervous gesture. Nico lay on the hospital bed, looking small and helpless, his gaze fixed on the ceiling. His brown hair was tangled and messy and his eyes red and bloodshot from the smoke.

"Physically, he's fine. For that we can be thankful." Dr. Brouwer looked over at Shannon, the Emergency Department nurse, who was also his wife. "Do you mind watching Nico for a moment?"

Shannon nodded, then gave Mia a comforting pat on her shoulder.

As Mia followed Dr. Brouwer out of the cubicle she shot another quick look at her son, but Nico kept looking up as if trying to find something on the ceiling.

As Ben Brouwer closed the door of an empty examining room behind them, he gave her a tentative smile that made her even more wary. "We've done all we can for Nico," he said, folding his arms and resting his hips against the door behind him. "The fact that he's not talking is not connected to anything physical. It's often called Selective Mutism. Sometimes that term applies to shy children, children who will speak at home, but not in public, or in Nico's case, children who won't speak after a stressful trauma. A counselor can properly diagnose this."

"So he might not talk again?"

"The mutism is generally temporary, but because it's psychological rather than physical we have no way of knowing how long it will last."

"So why is Josh okay?"

"Each child is different. Stress manifests differently in them. It might be Nico's way of controlling a world that, a few moments ago, fell apart for him in a dramatic and traumatic way. I would highly recommend seeing a counselor. I can set up an appointment with a Dr. Schuler in Cranbrook if you want."

Mia nodded. "Please. I want Nico to get help as soon as possible. And what do I do for him until then?"

"Give him peace and quiet. Return as much as possible to some type of routine. And don't pressure him to speak."

Peace and quiet. Mia could do with some peace herself, she thought, rubbing her chin again.

"Do you and your children have a place to stay?" Dr. Brouwer continued, his deep voice soothing. A good doctor's voice, Mia thought. "I understand from the paramedics that your apartment is unlivable."

She and her children had no place to return to. They had nothing but what they wore.

"Evangeline and Denny have offered us a place on the ranch," she managed to say.

But she wasn't sure she wanted to stay there. Nate

created emotions a mother of four children had no right to feel. Emotions she didn't dare let in her life again.

"I suggest you take the offer. Moving Nico away from town and away from the physical reminder of what he has just been through would be a good solution."

Mia massaged her forehead, the headache that had hovered at the back of her eyes all day now increasing. All she wanted to do was crawl into bed and retreat from thinking and planning.

Only her bed was probably a charred hulk.

Please, Lord, help me not to cry. Help me to focus on Nico. Please be with my little boy. Help me to get through all of this.

"I don't have a choice," she said quietly, her voice trembling in spite of her prayer. She waited a moment to compose herself then looked up at Dr. Brouwer. "Thanks so much for your time and your care. How is Jeff Deptuck?"

"He's okay. Some smoke inhalation but he'll be fine. Angie is with him now."

In spite of the circumstances Mia had to smile. Jeff had had a crush on Angie from the moment he met her. Every book club meeting he would alternately tease or flirt with her and for the most part, she seemed oblivious.

Guess it took rescuing her from a burning building to finally get her to notice him.

Just then another one of the ED nurses came to the doorway asking for him, and Dr. Brouwer pushed away from the examining room table. "Bring Nico and Josh to the office next week for a follow-up. Hopefully Nico will be back to his usual, chatty four-year-old self by then."

"I hope so," Mia replied. "Thanks again for all your help."

He laid a light hand on her shoulder. "You take care of yourself, as well, okay?"

Her only reply was a quick nod and then she followed him out of the room and back to the cubicle where Nico now sat, buttoning up his shirt. He looked up at her, then back down, his face still showing no expression.

"He told me he wanted to do it himself," Shannon said, giving Mia a quick smile.

"He talked to you?"

Shannon looked over at Nate, her expression holding a tinge of sadness. "He got his point across."

Mia's heart folded in on itself and she walked over to her boy, who looked so small on the large bed, and gave him a tight hug. "I love you, Nico," she murmured, resting her chin on his head. He still smelled like smoke. He needed a bath.

He leaned into her for the tiniest of moments, then pulled away, his fingers working at the stubborn buttons. Mia had to ball her hands into fists, so strong was the urge to help him.

When he was done she helped him off the bed. He clung to her hand and she squeezed tightly, trying to convey through her fingers as well as her words that she was there for him.

Then together, they walked down the hall toward the waiting room. The first person she saw was Nate, who got to his feet. He was still here, was the first thought that sang through her.

You shouldn't even be allowing him the tiniest space in your mind, was the one that followed on its heels.

"How is he?" Nate asked, holding her gaze for a heartbeat longer than he had to.

"The doctor said he'd be okay. We just need to come in next week for a follow-up, right, Nico?"

But Nico didn't acknowledge either by action or by word that he had heard what she said. He pulled free from her and ran directly to Nate and clung to him, burying his head against Nate's arm.

Nate looked from Nico to Mia and back to the little boy again, as if unsure of what to do.

"Nico, honey." Mia tried to lift the little boy into her arms, but Nico pushed her away. His shoulders shook, like he was crying. But he didn't make a sound.

Nico's hands scrabbled at Nate and finally Nate shifted himself around and hauled the little boy onto his lap. He patted him on the shoulder but Mia noticed that he was genuinely uncomfortable.

"It's okay," he muttered to the little boy, looking from him to Mia. "It will be okay."

Finally, after a long, uneasy moment, Nico's shoulders stopped shaking and he lifted his head. He looked directly into Nate's eyes, as if trying to find something there.

Mia laid her hand on Nico's shoulder but he still ignored her.

"Hey, buddy, you should go to your mom," Nate said with an awkward laugh.

Nico stared at him a moment longer, and this time he didn't resist when Mia took his hand and drew him away. But then Nico tugged his hand free, walked over to Josh sleeping on the couch and dropped beside him.

He drew his legs up to his chest then laid his head down. Retreating.

"I don't know what that was about," Nate said, slowly getting to his feet. "I'm sorry."

Mia waved off his objections. "Nothing to be sorry about." She was about to say more when Denny and Evangeline returned, each holding one of the twins, both of whom were fussing.

And as Mia looked at her children she felt a clutch of despair.

What was she supposed to do now? How was she supposed to take care of her children?

A sob clawed up her throat and she swallowed and swallowed, trying to fight it down. She couldn't break down. She had to stay strong. There was no one else for her children but her.

She dropped her face into her free hand, her fingertips pressing against her cheeks as if to restrain the fear and sorrow.

To her surprise she felt a large, warm hand rest lightly on her shoulder. Give it a gentle squeeze. "It's okay," Nate muttered. "It will be okay."

She wanted desperately to believe him but right now life overwhelmed her. A whimper crept past her tightly clenched lips.

No. Not now. Not in front of this man.

She stopped herself, took in a long, slow breath.

But no sooner had she released it then the overwhelming feelings of grief scraped away at her again.

A sob trembled through her, then another. Then Nate's arms were around her.

She fought his embrace but he held firm, his arms

strong and unyielding. Another sob broke free, then another. Then, all she could do was lean into him, let her tears flow and cling to him as the storm of sorrow and fear washed over her.

"Sorry I'm late," Nate said to Tango as he forked hay into the pen. "Can't believe I slept in that long."

He thought Denny would have woken him up when he headed out to drive his gravel truck this morning, but his brother seemed to think Nate needed the rest.

The roan stud stood in one corner, barely looking up when Nate approached.

"Hey, guy, how are you doing?" Nate asked as he opened the gate of the pen and stepped inside. He walked over to his horse, wincing at the sight of the cuts on the horse's face. "How's the leg?" he asked, gently running his hands down Tango's foreleg. Still warm, and still swollen. It would be a few days before Tango could put any weight on that leg. And probably even longer before he would be competing.

Nate stifled a sigh of dismay at the thought that all the work he had done with Tango, all the time he had spent training would disappear if he couldn't compete in the upcoming cutting horse competition in Livingston, Montana.

He gave Tango another pat on his withers then looked over the gate of the pen. His mare, Nola, stared back at him. Her large brown eyes seemed to accuse him. As it was all his fault they were in this dilemma.

"You'll be okay, girl," he said, his voice low and assuring. She had to be. The foal she was carrying was worth thousands. He beat down his nervousness, stacked his hands and rested his chin on top of them, watching Nola nose the hay he had forked to her earlier. He heard Bella nicker from the pen outside the barn and Jake's low, snorting reply. It was as if his horses outside were reassuring the ones inside, that all would be well. Trouble was, Nate wasn't so sure about that.

Nola turned around in her pen and he fought down a cough. Then another one. Socks, who had followed him into the barn, nudged his hand.

"Sorry, buddy," he said, coughing again, dropping to the straw-covered floor beside the dog, stroking his dark head. "That's what I get for trying to be a hero."

He rubbed his eyes, still sore from the smoke and fought down another cough as his thoughts circled back to Mia.

Last night, after coming back from the hospital, Nate had turned down Denny and Evangeline's offer of coffee and instead, had gone directly to the trailer he would be staying at. He needed some time alone.

It was disturbingly easy to resurrect the feeling of Mia's delicate body in his arms that moment in the hospital. How she had leaned into him and how easily his arms went around her. It had frightened him, but what bothered him more was how good it felt.

The tantalizing glimpse of something he couldn't— shouldn't—have.

He wanted to blame his reaction on the isolation that had dogged him the past few months. The feeling that, in spite of doing what he loved, there was a huge hole in his life. It was that feeling that had sent him back to reading the Bible. Sent him to his knees in prayer.

And now he would be on his foster brother's ranch for a while. But so would Mia and her kids.

What was he going to do about that?

The way she had depended on him, even for those brief moments, had created a blend of longing and fear.

Another fit of coughing overtook him and when it was done, he laid his head back against the rough wood of the pen. Socks laid his head on Nate's knee and he grinned at his dog, stroking his head. "I'll be okay, buddy," he said. "I survived my mom leaving me with Karl. This is nothing in comparison."

His mention of his stepfather reminded him of the letter folded up and stuffed in the back pocket of his blue jeans.

When he received the letter emblazoned with the name of a legal firm based out of Calgary he thought, at first, some mistake from the past had reared its ugly head. As he read the letter, he realized he was right.

His stepfather, the man who had put his mother in the hospital a couple of times and himself even more often, the man who had torn Nate's family apart and sent him into foster care, had died three months previous. And he had left all his money to Nate.

Nate unfolded the worn paper once again, the anger he thought he had dealt with rising up and threatening to choke him again. He didn't want any part of Karl Packer's money.

Blood money.

Guilt money.

As if giving him money would ever erase what Karl had done to him or his mother. There was no way he was taking it.

A rustling noise in the doorway of the barn made him shove the paper back into his pocket and get up. "Evangeline?" he called. Nate hadn't gone to the house for breakfast, but he was fairly sure Evangeline was also gone to work for the day.

But it wasn't his future sister-in-law who hovered in the doorway of the barn.

Nico stood there with a half smile and as he walked toward him, his eyes clung to Nate's, the same way they had yesterday in the hospital. He came to stop beside Nate and held out his hand.

Nate hesitated, not sure what Nico wanted.

I'm not that guy, he wanted to say to the little boy. *I don't dare give you anything. I don't dare let you into my life.*

Chapter Four

"Josh, Nico, we've got to get going." Mia gave Grace's face a quick wipe as she called up the stairs to the bedrooms above. Though Nico couldn't talk, nothing was wrong with his hearing and Mia knew he was playing upstairs in his bedroom.

While she set Grace beside Jennifer, Josh meandered down the stairs. His hair was still neatly combed and, thank goodness, his clothes were still clean.

"Josh, honey, can you speed it up a little?" Mia tried to keep her impatience from seeping into her voice as she stuffed a couple of diapers into the diaper bag that doubled as a purse and swung it over her shoulder. "We have a long drive ahead of us."

Ben Brouwer had pulled a bunch of strings, called in some favors and got her an appointment with the specialist today at 11:00 a.m. in Cranbrook, a fifty-minute drive away. "Is Nico coming?" she asked Josh as she picked up both twins.

"He's not here," he said in a matter-of-fact voice. "He went outside when you were in the bathroom. When you were changing Grace."

Panic streaked through her. There was a creek on the ranch. Nico loved water.

She charged outside, Grace and Jennifer bobbing on each hip, Josh barely keeping up with her. Her panicked gaze swept the yard when she got to the van. All she saw was buildings and fences. All she heard was the soft breeze in the trees surrounding the farmhouse. Denny was off to work and Evangeline had taken Ella to town for a doctor's appointment.

"Did he say where he was going?" Mia asked, setting Jennifer in one car seat, clipping her in one-handed.

"He's not talking, remember?" Josh said, giving her a frown.

Her mind raced as she ran around the other side of the van, secured Grace in the car seat and plopped a pacifier in her mouth.

"You stay here, sweetie," she said to Josh. "And don't move. Mommy is going to look for Nico."

Thankfully, Josh just shrugged, got into his booster seat and started playing the handheld Nintendo he'd found in the house.

She left the door of the van open as she called Nico's name, her voice sounding shriller each time.

"Nico. Where are you?" She called again, desperation filling her voice. *Dear Lord, don't let him be by the creek*, she prayed, one hand on her chest as she ran across the yard. *Please let him be okay.*

She paused a moment, listening again for something.

"He's over here."

Nate's voice. Coming from the barn beside the horse corrals.

Relief mixed with concern blended with a touch of anger. Why hadn't Nate brought him to the house?

She stepped into the barn, momentarily blinded as her eyes adjusted to the darker interior.

She blinked, looking around and then she saw Nico. He sat on the floor of the barn, leaning against the wall, stroking Socks's head. The dog's ears perked up when Mia came close and his brown eyes studied her, but he didn't leave Nico's side. Nor did Nico look up at her, his hand slowly stroking over the dog's head again and again.

Mia pushed her hand against her still-racing heart. A door creaked and Nate came out of a stall, looking surprised to see her there. "You okay?" he asked, his voice still hoarse from yesterday's smoke.

His hair was neatly brushed and his cheeks still seemed to shine from his recent shave. He wore a tan shirt today and clean blue jeans. If possible he looked even better than he had yesterday.

"Yeah. No problem. Just fine," she said with a dismissive wave of her hand, but she couldn't stifle her concern at the sight of her son here. Nico didn't bond quickly with people. His connection with Nate, though understandable, was worrisome, especially after listening to Denny talk about him last night. Turned out Nate was a loner who worked as a ranch hand over the winters and ran the cutting horse circuit all summer. A free spirit. Disconnected.

Certainly not the kind of man she could allow her children to become attached to. Especially not Nico.

"I didn't know Nico was here. I've been looking for him." Her panic was slowly being replaced by annoyance. "I'm leaving for a doctor's appointment in Cranbrook in a few minutes." She glanced at Nico, who seemed to be ignoring her. But she knew from the way his hand slowed its rhythmic petting of the dog that he hung on every word they spoke.

"Sorry. I didn't know," Nate said, closing the stall door behind him and latching it shut. "I would have sent him back to the house otherwise."

"I would appreciate it if you could do that next time he comes out here," Mia said, her request coming out more sharply than she intended.

"Sure. I get that." Nate reached for some lengths of rope and sat down on a nearby hay bale between her and Nico. "You heard your mom, sport," he said, addressing her son as he started to braid the three strands together. "You shouldn't come out here unless your mother knows."

"That's not what I was getting at." Mia lifted her head to hold Nate's dark gaze. For the tiniest moment an unexpected combination of fear and attraction thrilled through her.

Too easily she recalled how it had felt to be held by him. That surprising feeling of safety and support she hadn't experienced in a long, long time.

She swallowed and looked away, suppressing the foolish reaction, then squatted down in front of Nico. "Honey, we have to go. I need to be in Cranbrook in an hour."

Nico raised his head to hold her eyes for a scant second then shifted them to Nate, as if seeking his approval.

Mia fought down her agitation, aware of the other kids waiting in the van. The importance of making the specialist appointment hung over her like a cloud, yet right now she had to tread cautiously with her son.

So she placed her finger under his chin, to make

him turn his eyes back to her. Thankfully, he gave in right away and she eased off. "Sweetheart, I know it's nice to be here with Socks," she said, forcing herself to talk quietly. Slowly. Deflect the focus of his trip to the barn from Nate to the dog. "I know you love dogs, but right now Jennifer and Grace and Josh are waiting for us and I don't want Jennifer to start crying because she misses us."

Nico blinked and he opened his mouth and for a heart-stopping moment Mia thought he would speak. But his mouth worked, open and shut, but nothing. When she saw the shimmer of tears in his eyes, she drew him close. "Oh, sweetie, it's okay. You're safe."

She stifled her fear at how close she had come to losing him. But she couldn't stop herself from looking up at Nate, who watched them through narrowed eyes as his hands worked the rope.

He put the rope aside, crouched down beside Nico and laid his large hand on the boy's shoulder. "You should go with your mother, buddy. She needs your help right now."

Nico sniffed, nodded and then scrambled to his feet. He gave Nate a curt nod and, without another glance at Mia, left the barn, Socks trotting along behind him.

Though Mia was thankful for Nate's assistance it bothered her that Nico responded to Nate more than he had to her.

"Thanks for that," Mia said as she got up.

"Just trying to help," he said, holding his hands up in apology.

"I know that and I appreciate it." She hesitated, torn between her need to get going and her need to draw boundaries for her children.

Then he started coughing and her resolve wavered as she was reminded of what he had risked for the sake of her son.

He's not the kind of man you can let your children connect with. His leaving will cause Nico and Josh too much pain.

Annoying as she was, sometimes Other Mother was right.

"You know that I can't thank you enough for saving Nico's life," she started, watching as Nico stepped into the van.

"Please. Don't say any more. Anyone would have done the same."

"I don't know about that. However…" she hesitated, feeling ungrateful in spite of her words of thanks to him "…I am concerned about Nico and how attached he seems to be to you."

Nate's eyes narrowed and Mia wasn't sure how to read him. For the sake of her son, she kept going.

"Nico has a lot to deal with right now and I'm afraid that…that if he gets too attached, too connected, he'll get hurt when you go."

"Why do you say that?" His eyes still held her but his voice sounded grim.

"You're only here until your horses heal up, and then you're leaving, right?"

Nate nodded, affirming what she already knew.

"When my husband left, it took Nico a long time to get over that." For six months after Al had left, Nico slept with Mia, afraid to be on his own.

"And now the aftermath of this fire—" Mia's voice broke and she pressed her lips together, feeling an unwelcome jolt of sorrow for her family's loss of business and home. She looked away from Nate's piercing gaze, took a steadying breath and soldiered on. "I am worried that Nico is too strongly connected to you now. I don't want him hurt when you leave, so I would appreciate it if you could discourage him spending time with you, somehow."

The heavy silence following her request made her regret what she had said, but it was what she had to do to protect Nico.

"Sure. I get it." Nate looked away from her, bent over and grabbed the rope he had dropped. "You've got to take care of your kids. Keep them safe."

That was her only reason, she reminded herself as she hesitated, wishing she didn't feel like such a heel. "I know you rescued him and I can't tell you enough how grateful I am—"

"You don't have to thank me anymore," Nate said quietly, settling down on the hay bale, his eyes on the rope he was braiding. "We're good."

Mia hesitated a moment more, still not entirely happy with how things had gone down, torn between what Nate had done for her and what she had to do for her children.

He looked up at her and for the space of a heartbeat their eyes met. And for the space of that same heartbeat she felt it again. That glimmer of appeal. Of attraction.

Stop this. Quit this right now.

But she couldn't look away.

"You should go," Nate said finally, twisting the strands of rope together. "You don't want to be late."

She nodded her acknowledgement then without another word, left.

But as she walked across the yard to her van, she wondered if her warning to Nate was as much about herself as it was about Nico.

Chapter Five

Don't watch her leave. Keep your eyes on what you're doing.

But it was as if his practical mind and his lonely soul weren't communicating, and Nate watched Mia as she walked across the yard.

Her slender frame looked too fragile to carry the responsibility of four children, but he had seen the effect of the thread of steel running through her. The fact that she warned him away from Nico bothered him on one level and yet, at the same time, created a sense of admiration.

This was a woman who put her kids' needs first.

Something his mother never did.

He shook the foolish thoughts off, grabbed a pail of oats and headed outside to the corrals. He had been headed out to feed them when Nico had come into the barn. Instead, he'd had a one-sided conversation with the boy while he cleaned out Tango's stall. And then Mia showed up.

Nate poured the oats out for his other horses, spacing the piles far apart to keep them from fighting. Nola munched at her oats, lifting her head from time to time to make sure the other horses kept their distance. Nate walked around her, grimacing at the scratches that marred her golden coat. "Hey, girl," he said, running his hands over her expanding belly. "I'm excited to see your foal. Should be a real goer. But can you wait until we get settled in Montana before you have it?"

She nickered again, as if agreeing with him, then put her head down and continued eating, crunching at the oats.

Nate checked out the other horses, touching them, reminding them who was in charge. Before he entered the barn he stopped, looking behind him at the snow-capped mountains that edged the ranch feeling a twinge of envy at their beauty. His brother had ended up with a prime piece of real estate thanks to his deal with Evangeline's father, who had owned it previously.

He was happy for Denny, though. Nate knew how bad Denny felt after his divorce with his first wife cost the ranch that Nate had seen as a place of refuge. A place he felt safe. At the Norquests', he never had to worry about someone striking out at him for no reason. Locking him up in the basement for days on end.

And now, with the death of the man who had hurt and tormented him so often and in so many ways, Nate felt free. Though the letter tucked in his back pocket mocked that very freedom.

Nate spun around and strode into the barn, tossing the pail aside, struggling once again with memories that had, for the most part, been eased away with the unconditional love of Denny's family. They had introduced him to faith and had shown him a better way to live. His stepfather was nothing to him. He would take nothing from him. Ever.

Mia pushed the stroller back and forth, thankful the girls still slept, equally thankful she could get the large stroller into the counselor's office. Josh sat beside her immersed in his computer game. In the small room just off his office, she heard Dr. Schuler talking to Nico.

Please, Lord, let something good come from this, Mia prayed. She could use some good news. The girls were out of sorts and she knew a lot of it had to do with being yanked out of their routine. Josh was uncharacteristically cranky.

Tomorrow she had to deal with the insurance company, and her initial contact with the agent this morning hadn't been encouraging.

Please let the doctor have figured out how to help Nico.

The door creaked open and Dr. Schuler stepped out. With his blond goatee, longish hair, plaid shirt and faded blue jeans he looked more like a West Coast logger than a therapist. But Mia wasn't going to quibble about his wardrobe choices. Dr. Brouwer had had nothing but encouraging words for this man.

Nico came behind Dr. Schuler, clutching a handful of papers covered with the same colorful drawings as the papers Dr. Schuler carried. Mia suspected those pictures had been the main source of communication between them.

Dr. Schuler gave Mia a smile that she could only construe as encouraging. Then he stopped at his desk, laid the papers down and hit the intercom button. "Nancy, could you come into the office and take Nico and Josh to the playroom for a few minutes?"

A short, portly woman bustled into the office and squatted down in front of Nate and Josh. "I have a fun race-car set I would like to show you," she said.

Josh needed no encouragement, but Nico glanced at Mia, who nodded her assent. Only then did he leave.

"So I've had an interesting session with Nico," Dr. Schuler said as he tapped the stack of papers in front of him. "I understand both from Dr. Brouwer and from the pictures he made for me that he survived a fire?"

Mia nodded, her guilt over not being there plunging like a dagger in her heart as she clutched the stroller, pushing it back and forth, back and forth.

"It wasn't your fault, you know," Dr. Schuler said.

"I should have been there."

"With your two girls? Do you think you could have gotten four children out on your own?"

His probing questions put things into perspective for Mia. Reluctantly, she nodded, accepting the quiet wisdom he was giving her.

"Josh and Nico came through with minimal physical damage and for that you can be thankful. However, Selective Mutism is not uncommon in a child as young as Nico after a very traumatic event. It will go away, but it takes time and it takes giving Nico space to let us know what he wants."

"And what do you suggest?"

Dr. Schuler laid out the papers he had taken with him and leaned his elbows on the desk. "Could you have a look at these? Tell me if you recognize anything in them."

Though the pictures were crudely drawn, Mia had

seen enough of Nico's drawings to recognize what he was trying to portray. The first paper was covered with orange and red flames and in the middle of them stood a stick figure of a man wearing a black cowboy hat, a feather stuck in the band. The cowboy stood beside a smaller figure. The next picture beside it was of the same man, riding a horse. The man wore the same cowboy hat. Another picture showed, what Mia guessed, was the same stick figure. He stood by a horse, again, but a little boy rode the horse. Another picture depicted the same thing.

"Is there anything, other than the ubiquitous man with the black cowboy hat with the feather, that you notice about these pictures?" Dr. Schuler was saying.

Mia stifled a yawn as her eyes flicked over the pictures but she couldn't find what Dr. Schuler wanted her to see. "Sorry. My brain isn't working properly today."

"I'm sure it's had enough to think about. I just thought you might see something I might have missed. But I wanted you to notice two things. The man has all his features—face, eyes, nose mouth and hair. The little boy only has eyes. No mouth."

"Indicative of his lack of speech," Mia guessed.

"I would guess the same. And you can see that in each picture it seems to me the little boy is looking at the man. Is he familiar to you in any way?"

Mia slowly released her breath through pursed lips, thinking of Nico's actions of this morning. "A man named Nate rescued Nico from the fire. He's the foster brother of the man whose ranch I'm living on. He's a horse trainer and he's only passing through."

Dr. Schuler tapped his fingers on his desk, as if thinking. "You sound concerned."

"I am concerned about my son's attachment to him," Mia said, looking at the other pictures Dr. Schuler had brought along. All of Nate and Nico and horses. "This morning, before we came here, I found him with Nate in the barn. Nico doesn't form attachments quickly, so yes, it concerns me. It took him months to get over Al's defection. I can't afford to let him get attached to someone who will be leaving within the next couple of weeks."

"I understand. However, your son seems to have formed a strong connection to him and to his horses. I am presuming the connection with Nate started with the rescue from the fire. Now we just need to figure out how we can use it to help your son. So this is something you will have to deal with."

All that Dr. Schuler said reinforced Mia's own concerns about Nate, but it didn't negate the reality of Nico's connection to him.

"So what's next?" she asked.

"Another visit, obviously. We'll have to set up some type of schedule. This will take time and patience to deal with. As for the man in the pictures, is he trustworthy?"

The man had put his own life on the line to save Nico and Josh. He and Denny seemed to have a close relationship. Any of Mia's concerns about Nate and Nico were not because of Nate's character. But because of his circumstances.

"I believe he is," Mia said.

"Would you consider working with him and Nico. Possibly some supervised visits?"

"He lives at the same place we do. His brother owns the ranch we're staying at."

"Then having him spend some time with you and

Nico might be a possibility. He might be able to draw Nico out somehow. As well, given that Nico seems drawn to his horses, that could be another point of connection that you and this man could work with."

"We can figure out all we want," Mia said, "but if Nate isn't willing to help out, then we're no further ahead."

"If he's not, then we'll have to explore other avenues. Maybe the horses that also feature prominently in each picture could be a vehicle for his recovery. But for now, this man seems to be an important point of connection." Dr. Schuler leaned forward. "I fully understand your concerns and under any other circumstance I would feel the same. But to me Nico's mutism is wound up with this man. If, somehow, you could work with him and Nico, as well as his horses, we might see a breakthrough.

"If we can even simply establish a connection with Nico and the horses that might be enough to mitigate any concerns that might come up when this man, Nate, leaves. How do you feel about that?"

"I'm still not comfortable, but of course, I'll do anything for Nico."

"Of course you would," Dr. Schuler said with a smile as he leaned back in his leather chair. "You strike me as a loving and caring mother."

Grace started squawking and Mia jiggled the stroller to settle her down.

"One thing for next time—I would like to spend some time with you one-on-one during the next visit. You've been through just as much as the boys."

Mia waved off his concern as she turned the stroller

around to check on the girls. "I'm fine. I just need to get through the next few weeks."

Dr. Schuler gave her a thoughtful look, as if trying to see into her soul.

"Really. I'm okay," she insisted.

"The offer stands. Think about it."

"Thanks, but I'll be fine." She got up and slung the diaper bag over her shoulder. Thankfully, Grace had settled again.

"Stop at the reception area," Dr. Schuler said. "I'm fully booked up for next week, but hopefully you can get in after that. From there on we can set a weekly visiting schedule."

"Sure. Thanks so much for seeing me today. I appreciate you taking my son on such short notice."

"I look forward to seeing what we can do for him." Dr. Schuler got up and walked around the desk to the door to open it for her. "This is temporary. You need to know that. We can help your son. I am hoping this Nate man will be willing to help."

Mia's thoughts ticked back to the conversation she had just had with Nate this morning. How she had asked him to stay away from her son. Now Dr. Schuler was suggesting she ask for his help?

She thought of Nico and shook her head. One step at a time. For now, get home. Then you can figure out how to deal with this.

Chapter Six

"And how have you been feeling, Jeff?" Evangeline asked as she passed him a bowl of salad.

"I'm fine," Jeff said.

"You may be, but you're still a little hoarse." Angie glanced at Jeff sitting beside her at the long, wooden table in Denny's kitchen. Mia and her children took up one end, the adults the other. The full table reminded Nate of the dinners at the Norquests'. Lots of people and shared jokes, laughter and conversation.

Jeff just grinned at her as he heaped a generous helping of spinach salad on his plate. "A little hoarse? And here I figured you thought of me as a little puppy. Chasing after you."

Everyone groaned at that awful joke.

"We're thankful you and Nate could do what you did," Denny said. "And glad you both could join us for dinner. Our way of showing our appreciation."

"I know I can't thank you enough," Mia said quietly from her spot at the end of the table. "You and Nate."

Though she mentioned him as well, Nate didn't get a look like the adoring one Angie bestowed on Jeff.

"I understand you're out of your home, too," Angie said, turning to Evangeline. "When will you be able to open the store?"

"The insurance company will be done with their investigation tomorrow so I'm guessing in the next few days," Evangeline said. "I just wish Mia was having an easier time dealing with her insurance company."

"You get the service you pay for," Mia said, though Nate heard the frustration in her voice.

"Now that you and Jeff are here," Evangeline was saying, "what do you think about having book club here instead of at the store? We'll have to move the date by about a week, but would that work?"

"Sounds good to me. I love coming out here," Angie said.

"You could come, too, Nate," Evangeline said, drawing him into the conversation. "I know you read the book. I saw you taking it out to the barn this morning."

Nate shrugged her comment off but out of the corner of his eye caught Mia's surprised look. *Yes, I'm literate,* he wanted to say. "I'll think about it. If I'm still around." So much depended on Tango's recovery.

"And how was your visit at the therapist, Mia?" Denny took another helping of casserole, passing it on to Nate. He waved it off and passed it on to Jeff, who seemed to be enjoying everything that came his way.

Nate chanced a quick glance at the clock.

In spite of Jeff and Angie's company, dinner had been one tense ordeal he just wanted over. When Mia had come into the kitchen to see him there, her face fell. Then, when Nico had come to his side and leaned against him again, her eyes grew hard.

Wasn't difficult to imagine what ran through her

head. He eased Nico away, tried to make his excuses and leave, but both Evangeline and Denny had insisted he stay.

He knew it would look ungracious to refuse, so he stayed. But all through the meal he felt far too aware of Mia and Nico sitting across from him and the tension coiling her as tight as a filly.

"For a first appointment, it went pretty good," Mia continued, wiping some food off Grace's face. Jennifer was reaching out to Josh, who was laughing at her. "Nico drew a whole bunch of pictures. He did a great job." The look she gave her son created an unwelcome ache in Nate's heart. She managed to make each of her kids feel important and loved. His mother couldn't even do that with one kid.

"Did you want to show us your pictures?" Evangeline asked.

Nico shook his head, but then, to his surprise, looked over at Nate, his dark eyes intent. As if seeking something from him.

Sorry, buddy. Your mom doesn't want me near you and I don't blame her.

Nate wiped his mouth with the napkin. Time to go. "May I be excused?" he asked, picking up his plate.

"Of course, but we're not quite done." Denny pointed at the large book lying on the buffet against the wall of the kitchen.

Of course. Every evening after supper, Denny's family read the Bible and prayed. Nate felt foolish. Though he had been reading the Bible himself, he'd forgotten about this particular Norquest family ritual. So he sat down again, folded his arms over his chest, and while trying not to look at Mia, waited for everyone else to finish their dinner.

When everyone was done Denny set the Bible on the table and glanced around. "Evangeline and I have been reading from Romans," he said. "So I'll just carry on, if that's okay with our guests."

His question was purely rhetorical. No one said anything so he opened the Bible to the bookmark, cleared his throat and began.

"'In the same way, the Spirit helps us in our weakness,'" he read. "'We do not know what we ought to pray for, but the Spirit himself intercedes for us through wordless groans. And he who searches our hearts knows the mind of the Spirit because the Spirit intercedes for God's people in accordance with the will of God. And we know that in all things God works for the good of those who love Him, who have been called according to His purpose.'"

Nate's heart stilled as the words hooked into his heart. *God works for the good of those who love Him.*

He remembered Denny's mother saying those words to him as he sat, staring out over the ranch after telling her what he'd had to deal with at the hands of his stepfather. How she told him that if we trust in God, nothing in our life was wasted. He didn't believe her, but over time, as he fell into the rhythm of life on the Norquest ranch, he wondered if God hadn't used the circumstances of his life to bring him here.

Then the Norquests died and Denny got married and then divorced. The ranch was sold and Nate was on his own again with the bitter reminder of what happens when you let people too close.

A movement in the corner of his eye caught his attention. Mia had lifted her hand, pressing her fingers against her lips, furrowing her brows, as if she, too, was trying to figure out how God would work everything for her good. One of the twins, "Dimples," squawked and Mia immediately reached over and smoothed her hand over the little girl's head, an unconscious gesture.

Then, as if she sensed his attention, she looked over. He saw uncertainty in her expression and worry, and for a moment he wished he could ease all that away.

You're not that guy, he reminded himself. *You don't know how to take care of kids and she doesn't want you around hers.*

With a start Nate realized Denny had finished reading. He looked down and folded his hands, aware of the next step, promising himself, and God, that this time he would pay attention.

"Dear Lord," Denny prayed, "Thank You for this meal and that we could be here around this table safe and healthy. We continue to pray for Mia and her family. We ask that You will watch over them and restore them back to their home. Be with all of us who are searching for home. May we know that only in You, who works for our good, can we find our true home. Amen."

Nate kept his head bowed a moment longer, wondering if Denny was alluding to him with that last sentence. Nate knew he had drifted far from the faith introduced to him by his foster family. But he also knew the years he'd spent drifting around were an unspoken searching for a place he felt he could belong.

But not yet, he told himself. Not yet. He had goals he wanted to meet. Things he wanted to do.

Prove to your stepfather that you can actually amount to something?

Nate dismissed the pernicious thought as he got up from the table. His stepfather was dead and he didn't have to prove anything to anyone. He gathered up his and Denny's plates, and brought them to the sink where Evangeline was already working.

"Would you mind if I excuse myself?" Nate asked. "I want to check on my horses."

"They okay?" Evangeline asked. "I thought you spent most of the day with them."

"Yeah. But…" His excuse fizzled off as he looked over at Mia, who was watching him as if she was trying to figure him out. He held her gaze for a split second longer than he should have, feeling once again that faint quiver of attraction.

He turned back to Evangeline, who gave him an arch smile. "Of course. You go check on your horses. And you'll have to join us again for supper tomorrow."

Nate doubted he would. Hamburgers and pizza in Hartley Creek was probably on the menu until he could leave. And the sooner that happened, the better.

He slipped his cowboy boots on and stepped outside into the cool evening air. The sun was setting behind the mountains, pulling the warmth of the day with it. He took a long, deep breath, as if easing out the restlessness he could never completely shake and walked over to the barn. He just wanted to be around less complicated mammals. His horses didn't need anything.

He grabbed the book he'd been reading, the book club book that Evangeline had given him, settled onto a bale and made an attempt at reading. But he caught his eyes drifting off the page as his mind slipped back to Mia. Nico.

His own situation.

Though he understood why Mia didn't want him around Nico, it still created an edge of stress. He liked the little guy and felt sorry for him. He would have liked to help him, though he wasn't sure how.

Tango nickered, and Nate got up to see if he was okay.

His horse stood in the corner of the stall, his head down, obviously in pain. Nate stepped into the stall and walked toward his horse.

"Hey, guy. I'm sorry. If I'd paid attention I might have seen that camper before he cut us off," he said quietly and gently running his hands over Tango's leg, checking the injury. "I know you count on me and I let you down. But I'll help you get better and then we're out of here," he murmured. He gave Tango a final pat and stepped out of the pen.

Then startled as he saw Mia standing in the doorway.

She held a few pieces of paper in front of her, one corner of her mouth tucked between her teeth. The overhead light of the barn made her hair shine, made her eyes look larger and luminous.

Doe eyes, he thought, then dismissed the fanciful notion.

"Do you have a few minutes?" she asked.

"Minutes I've got lots of. You need some?" he asked, adding his own attempt at a grin. He seldom felt uncomfortable around women, but Mia put him on edge.

She held up the papers. "Nico drew these at our appointment with the therapist. I'd like your take on them."

Nate took the papers, puzzled as to what she hoped he could contribute. A chill fingered down his neck as understanding dawned.

"Something tells me that I'm the guy in these pictures," he said, flipping through them again.

Mia simply nodded.

"What is this supposed to mean?"

"Dr. Schuler thinks it shows a strong connection with Nico." Mia paused, pressing her thumbs together.

Nate handed her back the sheaf of papers. "I'm sorry, but there's nothing I can do about that. I promised you I would stay away from him and I will."

Mia bit her lip again as she took the pictures from him. "I realize that," she said, "and I appreciate it, but Dr. Schuler thinks…he thinks…that we should capitalize on this attachment."

Nate frowned at her. "What do you mean *capitalize?*"

Mia dropped down on the bale Nate had vacated a few moments ago, pressing the papers against her blouse. "He suggested that I talk to you about spending time with Nico. Spending time with Nico and your horses," she corrected. "He said that often horses are used in therapy situations. I know Denny doesn't have the time, and Dr. Schuler didn't think it would be as effective if it wasn't you working with Nico and horses."

"I can't believe this therapist wants me to spend time with Nico," Nate said. "I'm leaving as soon as my horse is better. Did you tell the guy that?"

Nate saw nothing but confusion in Mia's chocolate-brown eyes. "I told him and I know I'm still right. But Dr. Schuler thinks the advantages of you working with Nico will outweigh the disadvantages of you leaving."

Nate dropped his hands on his hips. "Doesn't matter what he thinks. I agree with you that I'm not the right guy for this."

"Why not?"

If he let himself get too caught up in this family, he would be too intertwined with Mia. Her kids.

"It's not a good idea," was his careful reply.

"I didn't mean to imply that you would hurt Nico on purpose. I just wanted to make sure his heart didn't get broken again. I was only thinking of his emotional well-being."

"So am I."

Mia looked down at Nico's pictures and one by one, flipped through them as a light sigh slipped out. "I can take care of kids who throw up, kids who are teething, kids with a fever, kids who hurt themselves. I don't know how to take care of this." She stopped, and once again she pressed her fingertips to her lips. Holding back her sorrow.

Nate suspected Mia had done this often in her life. Held back, stayed strong.

"I'm sorry," she said quietly, getting to her feet. "I hesitated asking because of what I said before. I feel so wishy-washy. I was just thinking of what's best for Nico." Her voice broke and Nate felt his heart flip.

He couldn't stop himself. He laid his hand on her arm, stopping her. She turned to him, hope flaring in her eyes.

"So what did this doctor want me to do?" The words spilled out before he could stop them. "How did he think I could help Nico?"

The relief on Mia's face eased his concerns.

"He told me that all you needed to do was let Nico spend some time with the horses. Ride them. Just be around them. Maybe he can help groom them if riding doesn't work out."

Nate pursed his lips and slowly exhaled. "Let me talk to the doctor and I'll give you a better answer tomorrow."

Mia nodded, her shoulders lowering as if she had been holding everything in until then. "That would be helpful. I'll give you his number," she said.

"I'm not promising anything," Nate said, still unsure this was the right thing to do. "I'll take this one step at a time."

"Of course," she said. "I realize that. Thank you. It doesn't have to be every day. Just when you can." She gave him a careful smile. A smile that didn't help his resolve one bit.

As she walked away, her slight figure receding into the gathering darkness, Nate knew he had to be careful the next few days.

Because leaving was the only thing he knew how to do and when he left, he wanted it to be with his heart and soul intact.

"So, I decided."

Nate stood in the doorway of the kitchen of Denny's house, his hands on his hips, his hat with the telltale feather tucked into the band pulled low over his head as if to hide his features.

Mia shifted Grace on her hip, her heart pounding in her chest with a mixture of apprehension and… anticipation?

She suppressed that last emotion. This was about Nico. She had to put her own foolish attraction to Nate aside. Yesterday, after she had talked to Nate about working with Nico, she was torn. Part of her hoped he would say no. Yet seeing how Nico had been attached to him, another part of her hoped he would help.

"What did you decide?" Mia injected a casual tone in her voice, thankful Evangeline was in the bedroom getting Ella dressed.

"I talked to the doctor this morning and he agrees that Nate would benefit from whatever supervised time I can give him." He dropped one shoulder and shifted his weight as if as uncomfortable about the situation as she was. "So I'll help Nico. As much as it's possible for me to in the time I'm here."

Her emotions did a cartwheel of gratitude followed by an unwelcome sense of anticipation.

"Thank you so much," was all she could say.

She could get through this. She just had to put her own foolish notions aside and keep her focus on her children.

"He said that you need to be there, too, and I agree," Nate added. "Besides the obvious propriety, your presence will create an overarching connection for Nico. For when I leave." He delivered that last sentence with a finality that underlined to Mia the utter foolishness of letting this man occupy even one tiny corner of her lonely soul.

"Of course. That makes sense." Dr. Schuler had hinted at the same thing.

"I know it will be hard for you, what with the twins and all." Nate's gaze slipped to Grace, who burbled happily in Mia's arms. Then he looked past her, took a few quick steps and grabbed Jennifer, who was standing up in her high chair. "Whoa, little girl. You almost fell."

"Sorry, I wasn't paying attention." Mia moved Grace to her other hip, holding out her free arm to take Jennifer from Nate. Guilt, a mother's steady companion, raised its ugly head again. As her mother, she should have been the one that caught her, not Nate. "You can give her to me."

"She's okay," Nate said, jiggling her in his arms. "Aren't you, Dimples?"

Jennifer chuckled and reached for his cowboy hat, knocking it awry.

"I'll take her," Mia insisted, holding out her arm.

Nate gave her an odd look.

"Of course you will," was Nate's enigmatic reply, but he gave her up, anyway.

Mia ignored his comment and set Jennifer on her other hip, adjusting their position so they were more evenly balanced. They seemed to get heavier each day. The time would come when she wouldn't be able to carry them both at the same time.

"So what time works best for you tomorrow?" Nate asked, stepping back, as if to give Mia some distance.

Mia mentally juggled her schedule. "The girls nap in the afternoon, so mornings will probably work best," she said. "Then I can take them outside with me in the stroller."

"Sure. Whatever will work for you. Or you could ask Evangeline to watch them," Nate said, shifting his cowboy hat back straight.

Mia shook that suggestion off. "Evangeline can't do it."

"Can't do what?" Evangeline asked as she slowly came down the stairs, leading Ella, who wore a bright pink, ruffled sundress, her fluffy sandy-colored hair pulled up into two ribbon-tied ponytails. Mia compared Ella's shining face and adorable outfit to her two ragamuffins. Her daughters wore oversize Onesies that had come in one of the many bags of donated clothes. Evangeline had given her what she could of Ella's hand-me-downs, but Ella had been dropped into Denny's life as a toddler and most of the clothes were still too big. All the twins' cute, matching clothes had been burned up in the fire.

The thought created another clench of loss. How many more times would she go through this, Mia wondered, feeling as if she was starting all over.

Though people had been helpful and generous, offering donations of furniture, bedding and household items, she didn't need much of what was offered as long as she stayed at Evangeline and Denny's. However, her other reality was all her memories, all her own "things" were lost to her. Pictures of the children, her computer, toys she had lovingly purchased.

She shook the maudlin thoughts off. She had other things to deal with right now.

"Mia is saying you can't watch the twins," Nate was saying to Evangeline.

"Of course I'll watch the girls," Evangeline said, her attention on Ella as the toddler carefully navigated the last step down. "I'm not going to town until later on this morning."

"Actually, I feel more comfortable taking the girls with me," Mia said, looking from Nate to Evangeline.

"Feeling a bit protective?" Evangeline asked with an understanding smile.

Mia nodded as she set the girls down. "And I'm sorry the kitchen isn't cleaned up yet."

"Don't be too hard on yourself," Nate put in, stepping past her to help her gather up the plates the boys had used. "Besides, isn't cleaning a house with kids like brushing your teeth while eating a chocolate bar?"

Mia shot him a quick look, then burst out laughing.

Her resolve started to drift. "It's your call about the girls," he continued. "If you take them out, you'll have to stay outside the corrals. I can't watch the boys, the horses and you."

"The boys?"

Nate nodded. "If we're doing this, we should include Josh. That way Nico doesn't feel singled out and Josh doesn't feel left out. It will seem more natural."

"That makes sense," she said, seeing the wisdom in his actions. "Thank you for thinking this through."

"Hey, I'm not just a pretty face," he said, carrying the plates to the counter.

Just then she heard the boys' bedroom door open. As they came down the stairs Mia wanted to close her eyes in pain. Josh wore a hot pink shirt with orange flowers paired with blue plaid pants. Nico, a neon yellow T-shirt emblazoned with the name of some computer game and orange jogging pants.

"Whoa, those are cheerful clothes," Nate said, humor threading his voice.

"We took them out of all those bags that the man and lady brought last night," Josh said, smoothing his hand over his shirt, beaming with pride.

"Do the boys have boots?" Nate asked Mia.

"No. Just running shoes," Mia said, glancing down at Nate's worn, slant-heeled cowboy boots.

"Boots for what?" Josh asked.

"Nate will be teaching you boys how to ride a horse," Mia said, breaking the news to them.

"Really? A horse?" Josh's grin almost split his face,

but it was the shine in Nico's eyes that dispelled any doubts Mia had.

"You guys will have to get your shoes on and we'll get you set up."

"A horse. We're going to ride a horse." Josh grabbed Nico's hand and without a second glance at Mia, ran out of the door. Mia was about to follow when Nate stopped her.

"I got the boys. You take care of the girls." His easy smile made his eyes crinkle and her stomach flutter.

Mia watched them leave, her heart hitching at the sight of the tall cowboy leading her two sons by the hand.

That should have been Al, she thought, though even as she formulated the thought she knew it was wishful thinking. Al had never been a hands-on father. Once in a while, if pressed, he would play with Josh, but seldom with Nico and, of course, he hadn't even seen his daughters.

"Looks cute, doesn't it?" Evangeline said, coming to stand beside her.

"Looks dangerous." The words popped out before she could stop them.

"Dangerous? How?"

Josh danced alongside Nate, his one arm waving as fragments of his chatter drifted back on the early-morning air. She saw Nate drop his head back as he released a deep belly laugh. Then he turned to Nico, his voice lowered as he spoke to her other son. Nate's dog, Socks, joined them, his plumed tail waving his joy, completing the Norman Rockwell picture.

"My boys are already too attached to him," Mia said,

the hitch in her heart deepening. "What am I going to do when he leaves?"

Evangeline's gentle sigh underlined Mia's concerns. "Like you've always said, just take it one day at a time," she said.

"I've tried to take it one day at a time," Mia returned, folding her arms over her chest. "But sometimes several days come flying at me at once." Then she gave Evangeline a smile. "But you're right. I need to take my own advice."

"I think he's a good guy," Evangeline said.

"And that's the trouble." And on that cryptic note Mia left to take care of her other children.

Chapter Seven

"I'm slipping. Help me, Nate," Josh called out from atop the horse he was riding.

Mia clung to the top rail of the corral, her other arm clutching Jennifer. She could do nothing but watch her oldest son clinging to the mane of the horse he was astride, slipping sideways off his saddle.

"Mom. Help," he called out.

This was a mistake, Mia thought. Josh was going to fall, get hurt and be even more afraid. He had survived a fire three days ago. How much more could he deal with?

Mia glanced back at Grace, who still slept in the stroller, and was about to climb over the fence, still carrying Jennifer when Nate called out. "I'm coming, Josh." Nate put Nico on his hip, then strode over to Josh's side and set him straight. "There you go, buddy. Good as new."

Josh took a few quick breaths, his eyes wide. "I got scared."

"I saw that," Nate said, patting him on the shoulder. "But you did good."

Josh gave Nate a feeble smile. "Really?"

"You really did. Most kids would have screamed and let go, but you didn't. You're a real cowboy." He turned to Nico. "Is it okay if I set you down, buddy?"

Nico nodded, his expression solemn.

Nate let him slide down to the dirt, but Nico didn't move from Nate's side.

"So let's see how we can stop that from happening again," Nate was saying to Josh. "First off, you have to make sure you don't lean to one side or the other. And see these?" Nate held up one of the stirrups, shortened to as far as it could go. "You have to keep your feet in these and the best way to do that is to keep your heels down. Not too hard or the horse will think you want him to go. Just enough that your toe isn't pointed down. That way your foot won't slip through the stirrup."

Nate gave Josh a few more pointers, his voice low, quiet, reassuring.

The horse Josh rode whinnied, shifted his feet and Josh wobbled again in the saddle.

Mia's heart jumped up her throat as Josh started sliding.

She was about to call the whole thing off, when she saw Josh grab the saddle horn, right himself and then, to her surprise, heard him laugh out loud.

Mia released her grip on the rail of the corral and let her own shoulders relax. Her son looked so small astride that huge animal. But Josh didn't seem as afraid as Mia knew *she* would be. Horses gave her the willies.

For the first half hour of the lesson Nate had introduced the boys to the horses and let Nico and Josh lead them around with a halter rope. He helped them with tight turns, wide turns, stopping and going. The horses were amazingly compliant, but it had been difficult for

Mia to watch her boys being followed by animals ten times their size and weight.

After that Nate had shown the boys the tack and what each piece did. Then he saddled and bridled the horses and got the boys to lead them around again.

Only then did he put them up on the animals.

Mia had watched the first part of the proceedings from her spot beside the girls sleeping in the stroller. But then Jennifer woke up and Mia had taken her out just when Nate put the boys on the horses. And all she could do was watch.

"So just sit right there and I'll get Nico on his horse," Nate said, "and then I can lead you guys around the corral, okay, cowboy?" Josh nodded. "You're doing great. Nola will stay where she is because she knows you're on top of her, okay? Remember how you led her around with the bridle? How you were the boss? You still have the reins and you are still the boss." Josh nodded and slowly his fearful look was replaced by a faint smile.

"All right, Nico. Let's get you settled on Bella." Nico's horse was smaller and had a much smaller saddle. Nate introduced Nico to the horse, Bella, let him pet her on the face, then asked if he was ready. Nico nodded. As Nate put Nico's feet in the stirrups and told him the same thing he had just told his older brother, Mia saw Nico listen intently, hanging on every word Nate said.

"Great. You make a good cowboy," Nate said, squeezing Nico's shoulder lightly. "Now I'm going to lead your horse toward Nola and Josh. Make sure you pet her once in a while so she knows she's doing a good job."

Nate caught the reins of Nola, Josh's horse, clucked to the animals and then led them slowly around the corral.

The ensuing silence was broken only by the rhythmic footfalls of the horses and Nate's low, reassuring voice.

And in spite of her own misgivings, an unforeseen peace fell over Mia's soul. They made a turn in the corral and Mia's heart expanded when she saw the wide smiles on both boys' faces and the excitement in their eyes. Nico was nodding in time to the gentle rhythm of the horse's hooves, his eyes flicking from his horse to Nate. A couple of times he patted Bella's shoulder, still grinning.

This was the most animated Mia had seen Nico since before the fire. And in that moment she felt the first tremble of hope.

"How are you boys doing?" Nate asked, walking toward Mia, looking back at them.

"This is so fun," Josh called out. "Look at us, Mommy. We're cowboys."

"You sure are," Mia said, giving them a small wave. Jennifer burbled and waved, as well.

Nate looked ahead and in the shadow of his cowboy hat she caught the glimmer of satisfaction in his eyes. He's enjoying this, too, she thought, surprised at the idea.

"You going to join us, Mia?" Nate said as they came closer.

"No, thanks. Me and horses…" She waggled her hand like an airplane to indicate her ambiguous relationship with the beasts.

Nate just grinned, his teeth a white slash in his tanned and dusty face. "Horses are a man's best friend."

"I thought that was dogs," Mia returned, looking down at Socks, who had lain quietly at her feet ever since Nate had pointed to the ground beside Mia and commanded him to stay.

"A dog won't take you up into the mountains," Nate said, still smiling. "Or carry your gear."

"A dog won't kick you," Mia returned.

"True enough." Nate grinned as he made another circuit of the corral. Then he stopped in front of Mia. "Hey, Dimples," Nate said. He touched Jennifer's cheek with one gloved finger. "You want to take a turn next?"

"You've called her that before. Why?" Mia asked.

"'Cause of the dimples at the corner of her mouth. And Grace has this cute nose. That's how I tell them apart."

Mia shot him a surprised look. "You can tell them apart? Most people can't."

"Can we go again?" Josh asked.

"I don't want you boys to get stiff and sore," Nate said. "So we'll make a few more turns around the corral and then you can go play."

Josh protested again.

"Honey, you have to listen to Nate—"

"We'll go again tomorrow—"

Nate and Mia spoke at the same time, stopped at the same time and exchanged a wry smile.

"Sorry about that," Nate said, giving her an apologetic look. "I didn't mean to cut in on you."

"That's okay." She returned his look with a smile.

And once again a connection rose up between them, as real and tangible as a touch.

Look away. Look away. Nothing to see here.

Other Mother's annoying voice cut in and the moment was shattered by reality.

She looked away, fussing with Jennifer just as Nate

turned and led the boys a few more times around the corral. She set her little girl in the stroller beside her sleeping sister and turned them away from the sun, pushing the stroller back and forth to keep Jennifer quiet.

Jennifer squawked a few more times but then Socks stood up, looking over the edge of the stroller, his tongue out, his soft eyes looking so friendly. Mia had to smile and Jennifer started laughing.

Nate's animals—keeping my kids happy and entertained, Mia thought, shooting another quick look over her shoulder at Nate. He was tying up the horses, joking with the boys, telling them silly stories.

He puzzled her. The first time she met him he seemed turned off by the fact that she had kids. When Nico had glommed on to him at the hospital, he looked genuinely uncomfortable.

Yet here he was, chatting with Josh and Nico like he had known them forever and was able to tell her girls apart. Something not even Evangeline, one of her best friends, could do.

"Mommy, did you see me? Could you see me? Did you take a picture?" Josh clambered over the fence, his words spilling out in a stream of pure joy.

"No, honey, I didn't take a picture." Another loss squeezed her heart. Her camera, and the past year's moments had been lost in the fire.

"But you always take pictures," Josh said, puzzlement threading his voice.

"I know, honey, but my camera—" And goodness, if her voice didn't break just as Nate and Nico climbed over the fence to join them.

She gripped the handles of the stroller, determined

not to show her weakness in front of this man, who was slowly taking up space in her mind. And then she felt his hand on her shoulder, as if he understood what she was grieving.

She swallowed, then swallowed again.

"So, boys, we're done. Why don't you go and play?" Nate suggested, his deep voice quiet.

To Mia's surprise they simply nodded and ran off, Josh still talking excitedly about their adventures of the past hour.

"Are you okay?" Nate asked.

Mia waved off his concern, but to her consternation, he kept his hand on her shoulder, squeezing lightly. "I keep forgetting how much you lost in that fire," he said.

She released a hard laugh. "Everything but the clothes on our backs, the stuff I had in the girls' diaper bag and my minivan." Then she caught herself, and drew in a long, slow breath, centering herself on what was important. "I'm thankful for what I have and I'm thankful for the support I've gotten from my friends. God is good."

Nate's brows lifted in surprise. "You can say that in spite of everything that's happened to you?"

His mouth quirked up in an uncertain smile.

"He is," she returned. "Things haven't been great and I've questioned what has happened to my life, but through it all I've felt God near me, supporting and strengthening me."

Nate's eyes narrowed. Seemed to sink back and retreat. "That's a blessing. I wish I could say the same with as much conviction."

She caught the tail end of an old bitterness in his

voice. A resignation toward some past event. "What do you mean?"

Nate seemed to contemplate her gentle probing. Then he shook his head. "Doesn't matter. I better go take care of the horses."

He vaulted over the fence in one easy motion, striding toward his horses, his gait full of purpose.

But she guessed from his abrupt movements, the faint slouch of resentment in his shoulders, that what was "done" hadn't been completely eradicated from his life.

She knew he was a foster child. It didn't take much of a step to presume that the reason he'd been put into Denny's family haunted him still.

Don't delve into his life. You've got enough going on in yours.

Mia knew that this time Other Mother was right.

As she walked away, pushing the stroller over the rough ground, she couldn't help a quick glance over her shoulder.

She was dismayed to see Nate, clutching the reins of the horses, watching her, his features shadowed under the brim of his hat.

"Easy, Sierra." Nate clucked to Denny's horse. He nudged him in the side, urging the large chestnut bay through the gate leading from the cattle pasture to the horse pasture. Sierra balked and spun around as if to go back to the cows they had just checked on. As Nate turned him around to face the gate again.

Sierra turned, as if to head back to the horse pasture to join the other horses. "You need to learn some manners," Nate said, making the horse stay. Sierra tossed his head and jumped, but Nate kept firm control of the reins. "I'll need to work with you later," Nate warned as he finally let him go back to join his and Denny's two other horses.

This morning Mia hadn't come to help him with the boys, which suited him just fine. He needed space from her. Space to center himself.

He knew helping Nico would be a complication for him, but how could he say no when the kid needed so much? When the boy's mother could use every bit of help sent her way? But he hadn't counted on the attraction that sparked between him and Mia when they were together. It was as if she filled a place in his heart he hadn't known was empty until he met her.

And that scared him.

He dismounted, quickly unsaddled Sierra, brushed him down and then led him back to the pasture where the other horses whinnied in greeting.

He tugged his truck keys out of his blue-jeans pocket and checked his shirt pocket for his cell phone. A quick brush of his hands over his pants and he was ready to go. He didn't figure on being back at the ranch until after supper again.

He climbed over the fence separating the horse pasture from the ranch yard and strode across the packed dirt, swinging his keys on his index finger.

And then he came to a stop.

Mia's van was still parked on the yard. She was supposed to have been gone by now.

But the hood was up, the sliding door open. And he could hear one of the girls crying. Obviously, something was wrong.

Denny was still working and Evangeline's car was gone, as well, so it was up to him to find out what.

Tamping down his own misgivings, Nate hurried over. From this point all he could see were Mia's legs in the front of the van, the rest of her bent over the engine.

"Nate. You are here," he heard Josh call out from the inside of the van.

Mia pulled back so abruptly she banged her head on the hood. She cried out and grabbed her head, then grimaced as she looked at Nate.

"You okay?"

Mia winced, then rubbed her head. "Yeah. I'm fine. But something's wrong with the van. When I started it the oil light came on. Which doesn't make sense because I just got an oil change on it before…before the fire."

"Did you turn it off right away?" Nate asked, pulling the dipstick out.

"Yeah. I didn't dare let it run."

"Smart girl," he said, wiping the dipstick off on the lower edge of his pant leg. He slipped the dipstick back in, pulled it out again, but nothing registered. Strange.

He bent down to look under the van and then he saw a greasy spot of oil on the dirt. He crouched down and looked up into the engine. "I see the problem. There's no oil plug in the line. All the oil has drained out."

"But I drove it to the therapist the other day."

"The plug was probably not put in properly and jiggled loose on the road back into the ranch," Nate guessed. "Good thing it didn't happen sooner or you would have seized up the engine and been stranded halfway between here and Cranbrook."

Mia pulled her hand over her face, releasing another sigh. "This is not good."

"You needed to see the insurance guy today, didn't you?"

"He's leaving tomorrow and won't be back in the office until next week Wednesday. I need to get my claim started as soon as possible. I can't keep staying here at the ranch."

"I'm sure Denny and Evangeline don't mind having you here," Nate said, tightening the dipstick and closing the hood of the van, the clang of it reverberating over the yard with a sense of finality.

"I know they don't," she said, releasing a sigh. "But they have Ella, and Evangeline does enough running around back and forth to town every night. As well as having her own stuff to deal with from the fire and they're planning a wedding. Me and my four extra blessings definitely complicate things for them."

"But your kids are such cute blessings." As soon as the words left his mouth he felt like doing a face palm. Not the way to keep your distance, Lyster.

But it earned him a smile from Mia. "I think so but I'm prejudiced." And then she looked at her kids and in spite of all the stuff that life had thrown at her, Nate saw a gentle smile curve her lips.

She didn't resent the presence of these kids in her life one iota. Not a jot.

He wiped his hands again and looked at the kids, then at his truck parked by his stock trailer across the yard. It was a double cab and if they squeezed, they could put the car seats and one of the kids in the back. The console in the front flipped up, which meant Josh could sit there.

"I have to go into town," Nate said. "I could take you."

Mia's shake of her head was automatic. Nate knew that by now. "No. It's okay. I'll just go next week."

"You need to get things started as soon as possible," Nate said. "I'm going, anyway. Give me a few more minutes and we can get the kids moved around."

Mia was about to shake her head again and then he saw her pull in a deep breath of resignation. She shot him a look of sheer gratitude, but still seemed to feel the need to add one more token protest. "Are you sure?"

Nate didn't even bother replying. He pulled the van door open and asked Nico and Josh to come out. "You take out Grace's car seat, I'll catch Jennifer's," he said to Mia, looking down at Jennifer, who was grinning a drooly smile. He grinned back at her. She waved her hands and giggled and he felt a curious hitch in his heart.

Again, enough. He unbuckled her car seat and carried her, seat and all, back to his truck.

Fifteen minutes later the kids were all buckled in and they were on their way. Five minutes into the trip the twins fell asleep and Nico sat quietly, playing with the old Nintendo.

"This is a great day," Josh said, sitting up straight, his eyes glued to the road as if he had never seen it before. "I got to ride a horse and I get to sit in the front of Nate's truck."

"Mr. Lyster," Mia gently corrected.

"I don't care if he calls me by my first name," Nate said, waving off her protest. "Mr. Lyster sounds like a character from a kid's book."

"Why do I have to call him Mr. Lyster when you call him Nate?" Josh pressed.

"Because it's polite, that's why," she explained in a patient voice.

"Now I feel old," Nate joked.

"You're hardly old," Mia returned. "I'm sure you still buy green bananas."

Nate chuckled at that. "The few times I go grocery shopping."

"I understand you don't have your own place?"

"I mostly rent when I need to stay in one place for a while to work with the horses. I think the last place I called home was the Norquest ranch."

"How long were you there?"

"I moved onto the ranch when I was twelve. Stayed there until Denny and Lila got divorced and Denny had to sell the ranch."

"Is that when you started working with cutting horses?"

"I started before that. Before I got to the ranch."

"Did the Norquests raise cutting horses?"

Nate leaned back, his wrist resting on the top of the steering wheel as he slipped back to the past again. "Nope. Karl did. My stepfather."

Mia was quiet a moment as if digesting this information. As if trying to figure out the convoluted path Nate's life had taken to end up at the Norquests'. He wasn't about to tell her.

"So what does a cutting horse do?" she asked, thankfully veering away from that topic.

"You got ten hours?" he asked, slanting her a grin.

"Twenty-four minutes," she returned.

He just laughed, surprised how easy she was to be around. "It's not that interesting."

"I'm interested," Mia put in. "Tell me."

"Basically, a cutting horse is used to cut animals out of the herd when they're out on pasture. If you have a calf you want to vaccinate, or a cow you want to check, a cutting horse can separate them and get them where you want them. It's how animals were handled out on the open range and still are on the larger spreads. Over the years it turned into a competition. That's what I do."

"And how do you do that?"

"Well, that's where the ten hours of explanation comes in."

"Mommy, I'm tired," Josh said with a yawn.

"Just lay your head on my lap, honey."

"Told you it wasn't interesting," Nate said.

"Busy morning for him." Mia stroked his hair out of his eyes. "By the way, thanks again for working with the boys. That's all Josh could talk about afterwards."

And all Nate could think about.

"No problem," he said. "They're good boys. You've done well with them." He shot a quick glance back at Nico, who looked intent on the Nintendo, but Nate sensed he was listening to every word.

"It's never enough. I love my kids and I'd like to be the ideal mother, but I'm too busy raising them."

"That covers a lot, in my books," Nate said with a wry note in his voice. "And I think you're doing okay. No. That's wrong. Considering your circumstances, you're doing amazing."

Mia gave him a quick smile, then looked ahead, but Nate saw a faint flush reddening her cheeks as she fingered Josh's hair away from his face. Was she embarrassed?

"That's sweet of you to say so."

That was him. Sweet as candy floss. And as long lasting.

Nate forced his attention back to his driving. Being around Mia seemed so easy in one way and yet complicated in another. He shot a quick look at Josh, then his eyes flicked up to Mia.

Only to find her looking at him.

He quickly tore his gaze away the same time she averted her eyes, as well.

Silence sprawled between them, filling the space in the cab. And the rest of the way to town, though Nate kept his eyes on the road, his attention was split between his driving and Mia's gentle movements of her hand on Josh's head.

"Where do I need to drop you off?" Nate asked finally as he turned off the highway and into the town.

"On Fernie Avenue, just off Main," Mia said, gently shaking Josh to wake him.

He nodded but then, as he turned onto Main Street, he felt a clench of dismay as he saw the blackened hulk of what was once Mia's flower shop and home. Menacing sheets of dark soot stained the brick front and the windows stared like vacant eyes, their glass broken and shattered. The front door was boarded up, creating a sense of finality. This business was over. Done.

"Oh, dear," Mia whispered beside him as they drove past. "What a mess."

"Are you allowed to go in?"

"Jeff Deptuck called me yesterday. Said it was safe to look through the main floor but that the upstairs was

off-limits. I was hoping to see if anything was left..."
Her voice faltered and she drew in a shaky breath.

"Are you sure you want to?"

"No, but I feel I should."

"We can go after you see the insurance guy. I'll come
with you."

Mia gave him a grateful look. "That would be nice.
I'll see if Evangeline can watch the kids. I don't want
them to see their old home."

Nate acknowledged that with a quick nod as he
turned onto Fernie Avenue and parked the truck.

"I'll get the stroller," he said. "You take care of the
kids."

And before Mia could protest he was out of the truck
and pulling the collapsed stroller out of the box. He
tried to unfold it but the various latches and hooks con-
founded him.

"Having trouble?" Mia asked, a note of humor in her
voice as she came beside him.

"I'm sure a woman invented this thing just to tick
men off," he grumbled.

Mia chuckled, took it from him and with a nudge of
her toe, a flick of her thumb and a quick shake, it unfolded, neat as can be. "Nothing to it," she said.

"I guess." He sighed. "And here I was hoping I could
help you."

She patted him on the back like she would one of
her kids. "I appreciated the thought." She went to get
the girls, but this time Nate was one step ahead of her.
He carefully unbuckled Grace, who, surprisingly, still
slept, and lifted the warm bundle of little girl out of the
seat. She scrunched up her face, twisted in his arms

and then, when he set her in the stroller, sighed and fell back asleep again.

"Amazing how these girls can sleep," Nate said in admiration as he buckled the little girl up.

"It's been a blessing, that's for sure." Mia set Jennifer in the stroller beside her then tossed the diaper bag into the bottom basket. "Okay, boys, we should go."

Nate imagined those poor boys sitting in a stuffy office while Mia dealt with the insurance agent. He made a quick decision and before he could change his mind said, "Why don't I take them with me?"

"No. You have your own things to do."

"I just need to pick up some parts from the hardware store."

Nate knew from the way she wrinkled her nose she was going to protest again. He crouched down in front of Josh and Nico, pushing his hat back on his head as he preempted her. "So, boys, do you want to come with me and see some fun stuff or do you want to go with your mommy and listen to an insurance agent talk for hours about liabilities, appraisals and comprehensive insurance coverage?"

"Huh? We want to come with you," Josh said. "Right, Nico?"

Nico added an enthusiastic head nod.

Nate shot Mia a triumphant glance as he straightened. "Guess the hardware store trumps the insurance office."

He could see her formulating another protest, then she shook her head as if giving in. "Okay. I guess. But as soon as they misbehave—"

"I'll take them to Hartley Creek and dunk them in.

Headfirst," Nate said, grabbing Nico as if he would do so right now.

Nico's shoulders shook and for a moment, just for a bright and shining moment, Nate thought he would laugh out loud.

But he didn't.

Then Mia bit her lip and he wanted to put his arm around her and console her. Yet common sense prevailed and instead, he set Nico down on the sidewalk.

"C'mon, boys. Wave goodbye to your mom. We got to get going." He looked over at Mia again. "Text me when you're done."

"Thanks so much," she said quietly.

Their gazes meshed and Nate felt that flicker of appeal again. He gave her a curt nod, took the boys' hands and left.

The hardware store wasn't busy and Dan, the owner of the store, was helpful and knowledgeable.

"Those Mia VerBeeks's kids?" Dan asked as he bagged Nate's purchases.

"Yeah. I'm watching them while she gets her insurance stuff figured out."

"Too bad about what happened. I hear the boys barely got out with the clothes on their backs."

Nate glanced down at Nico and Josh, noticing Josh's too-short pants and how the oversize T-shirt hung on Nico's narrow shoulders and thought of their running shoes they wore riding. "Is there a place I can get some kids' clothes?" he asked as he took the bag from Dan.

"Family Fashions, just down the street, is your best bet."

"Thanks. I'll check it out."

He called the boys and together they walked down the street and into the store Dan had pointed out to them.

Nate stood inside the doorway looking around, not sure where to start.

A young woman, medium height, her blond hair pulled back in a bouncy ponytail, approached him with a friendly smile. She wore a pink T-shirt and white flowy skirt. The type of skirt Evangeline liked to wear. "Good afternoon. My name is Lacy," she said, her eyes flicking from Nate to the boys and back again. "Hey, Nico. Josh. What can I do for you all?"

Nate rested his hands on the boys' shoulders. "I'm looking for cowboy boots for the boys," he said. "And some clothes."

"Really? For us?" Josh squealed. He grabbed Nico's hand. "Cowboy boots!"

Lacy gave the boys a benevolent smile. "Let's go to the back of the store where the shoes and boots are, and we'll start with that."

Nate followed along behind the boys, who were dancing with excitement.

Shoes and leather boots of various shapes and styles decorated the wall and Nate caught the familiar and comforting scent of leather.

Lacy measured the boys' feet and then looked over to Nate, gesturing to one section of the wall that held boots and running shoes and sandals in smaller sizes. "Why don't you and the boys pick some boots out and I'll see if we have them in stock."

Nico was already on the floor, tugging on the ugly running shoes he wore. He dropped them with a thump on the carpeted floor and bounded to his feet to follow his brother.

"What price range are you looking at?" Lacy asked as they joined the boys who stared, wide-eyed, at the selection.

Nate waved off her question. "Doesn't matter. I want to get them good boots."

"Okay, let's see what we can find."

"I wish Mommy could be here," Josh was saying as Nate helped him choose a pair of black boots with bright red stitching.

"Where is Mia?" Lacy asked. Nate easily heard the curiosity in her voice.

"She's settling stuff at the insurance agent. I thought I would give her a break and take the boys."

"That must be so hard for her. And with all those kids." Lacy shook her head, her ponytail bobbing in commiseration. "I always thought it was so awful how Al left her when he found out she was expecting twins. Not that it mattered that much. He wasn't such a nice guy. He was always flirting."

Nate took the boot Nico was showing him, his mind trying to wrap itself around this information. Part of him, the part curious about Mia, wanted to ask more, but knew Mia wouldn't appreciate the chatter.

Instead, he turned his attention back to the boys. "Are these the ones you want, Nico?" he asked, holding out the brown boots with the green shaft.

Nico nodded, his eyes shining, his mouth open.

Nate waited a moment, his heart vibrating in anticipation, but Nico just stood there. Silent.

"Okay. I guess they've made up their minds," Nate said, handing Lacy the boots.

She took them, holding his gaze longer than he thought necessary and then, thankfully, she left. She returned a few minutes later with a stack of boxes. "I took a larger size for each of them. Just in case," she explained as she set the boxes on the floor and opened the top one.

Nate helped Nico get the boots on, and when the boy stood, Nate didn't think he could smile any more.

"Mine fit. Mine fit," Josh called out, bounding to his feet, holding them out for Nate's inspection.

"They look great," Nate said, grinning at the boy's enthusiasm. But at the same time his heart ached for Nico, stuck in his silence.

Nate bent over to take the boots off, but Nico pulled his foot back, shaking his head.

"They can wear them right away if they want," Lacy said, taking the boys' ratty running shoes and setting them in the box the boots came in.

Nate shot her a thankful look. "I don't think we're getting them off."

Lacy just beamed.

"Now some clothes," Nate said. "Some blue jeans and shirts."

"Of course. I can show you where they are."

Josh grabbed his one hand, Nico, the other, and bracketed by these happy, thrilled boys, Nate felt a thrum of joy followed by a sudden uncertainty.

What was he doing? He was leaving in the next few weeks. He had to.

Or did he?

Chapter Eight

It was beyond disaster. Beyond incomprehensible.

Mia stood in the back room of her flower shop, her arms clasped over her midsection, as if holding her emotions inside.

Charred and blackened timbers held up a roof with exposed beams. Fixtures with broken glass hung from bare wires dangling from the ceiling. The floor was a mass of soot and water stains covered with remnants of drywall. The door of the walk-in fridge that had held her flowers hung drunkenly on one hinge, melted containers and buckets scattered over what was left of her worktable and the floor.

"You don't have to see this." Nate spoke quietly beside her, his own expression shuttered. Mia wondered if he was reliving that moment when he ran into this very building when it was ablaze.

"I had hoped I could salvage something," she said, her voice small and weak. "Anything."

"Don't think there's much left here."

"And I'm not allowed to go upstairs." Where all her important stuff was. Clothes, jewelry handed down to her from her grandmother. The fine china her parents had bought her as a wedding present.

"There's probably not much left there, either," Nate said quietly.

Mia looked around again, thankful she had brought the children to Evangeline. She didn't want them to see what had become of their home. Her store.

How was she supposed to carry on? This store had been her salvation. It had taken her through those dark days when she was alone, pregnant with the twins and responsible for two young boys.

A faint sob crawled up her throat. She fought it down, swallowing again and again.

The kids need you. You have to stay strong.

This time Other Mother was right. Mia pulled in a shaky breath, but then felt Nate's hand on her shoulder. Why was this man always around at these difficult times? She was about to turn away when a breeze sifted through the building and a piece of paper floated down from a room above.

One corner of it crumbled to ash as Mia, curious to see what it was, picked it up. She turned it over and her heart stuttered over its next beat.

Nico and Josh grinned at her, each of them awkwardly holding a baby. The girls were crying, their faces scrunched up under the frilly brims of bonnets that had been a gift from Mia's mother.

Mia's hand trembled as her fingers traced the children's features. She had hoped to make a scrapbook of her children's photos one day. Her friend, Renee, who owned a scrapbook supply store, was going to help her.

And now…

Mia clutched the picture as tears welled up in her eyes, blurring her children's features.

"It's all gone," she said. "Everything I have."

The true devastation of the fire hit her right then. Her world had sharply tilted and she was doing everything she could to keep her feet underneath her. She faltered, reaching back to steady herself and then, once again, she felt Nate's arms around her. She knew she should pull away. Stand on her own two feet. But she allowed herself to stay a moment longer in the strength of his embrace. Allowed herself the feeling of having someone hold her, support her. Be strong for her.

But even as she leaned against him, a more practical and insistent voice took over.

He's leaving. He can't supply your needs.

It was that last comment that made Mia straighten. Made her look away as she drew in a wavering breath.

When Al had left, Mia had sat on the floor of her bedroom, her Bible in her lap. She had prayed, read and prayed some more. It was in that moment that she came to the realization that the only one who could supply all her needs was her Savior, Jesus. No man could do that for her.

Nate couldn't do that for her.

Then, just as she had centered herself spiritually and emotionally, she felt the gentle brush of Nate's lips on her forehead.

He was just consoling her, she told herself.

Then why did that light touch make her heart race?

She took a deep breath as she slowly pulled back from him, looking at the devastation surrounding her as if to imprint it into her mind. Remind her of what her priorities were.

"We should go." And without a second glance at him, she turned and walked out of what was left of her flower shop. Back to her children, waiting for her. Back to her real life.

"You're looking pensive," Evangeline said as she dropped the last dish in the dishwasher. Supper was over. The children were all in bed and the house was quiet. "Are you upset that Nate didn't join us for supper?"

"No. Of course not." Even as Mia dismissed Evangeline's prodding question, her hand crept up and touched her forehead where Nate had kissed her. She still wasn't sure if she had imagined it or if it had actually happened.

At the same time she was thankful he had stayed away.

"But something is bugging you," Evangeline pressed, folding her arms over her chest in her "I mean business" gesture. "You're all squirrely."

Mia realized Evangeline wasn't going to quit and as she glanced at the carrier bag from Family Fashions, hanging from the stairs' banister, she chose to home in on that. Distract her friend with the other thing that did concern Mia.

"I don't know what to think about the stuff Nate bought the kids," she said. The bag not only held blue jeans, a couple of plaid shirts and a few T-shirts for the boys, it also held a couple of ruffly dresses. One in pink and one in green and half a dozen sparkling white Onesies and some sleepers.

The boys were wearing the boots when they joined

her and Mia had to pry them off their feet before bedtime.

Evangeline gave her a sly smile. "Cut the tags off?"

"Be serious. It's too much. I don't know what to do with it all. It makes me uncomfortable."

"How?"

"It's like I can't take care of my own kids." Which was only part of her discomfort. The other was the shift in her and Nate's relationship.

"I'll tell you what you're going to do with those clothes." Evangeline grabbed Mia's hands, giving them a light shake. "Take them out tomorrow and let the boys wear them. Save the little dresses for the girls to wear to church on Sunday. You're going to let this kind and generous man give your kids a gift."

Mia pressed her lips together, reining in her protests, realizing how ungrateful she sounded.

"You are allowed to let people do things for you," Evangeline continued, laying one hand on Mia's shoulder and giving her a light squeeze. "You would do the same for anyone else if they needed your help."

"But that's different—"

"It's not different." Evangeline cut her off. "Just because he's a guy doesn't change anything. He wanted to get your kids something. I know you have a hard time taking things. You're so independent. But sometimes you have to let people give things. For *their* sake."

Mia realized the truth of what Evangeline said. She did have a hard time accepting help, let alone gifts. But still…

This was Nate, not a member of her church or community.

Yes, it was generous of him to give her boys these

clothes, but tangled in that was what happened at her store when she leaned on him. When she felt his gentle caress.

"You still don't think you should accept this, do you?" Evangeline said with a teasing smile.

Mia's innate sense of self-preservation kicked in. But weariness and exhaustion also clawed at her with a relentless hunger. She had few reserves left to carry the load she'd been lugging around since Al left her.

"I'm scared," she said quietly, the admission, spoken aloud, increasing the emotion. "I'm scared of what's happened the past few days."

Evangeline, still holding Mia's hand, pulled her down to the kitchen chair behind them and sat down across from her. "Of course you are. It's been huge."

"It's not only the store," Mia said, blowing out a sigh. "It's Nate. I don't know if I'm overreacting to him or if I'm reading too much into simple actions."

"What actions?"

Mia pulled her hands away from Evangeline's, twisted her fingers around each other and let her hands rest in her lap. Her broken nails and rough hands mocked her. The hands of a florist.

Not anymore.

"Right now, Nico needs me a lot. Trouble is, according to Dr. Schuler, he also needs Nate. And it's scary how quick Nico has attached himself to Nate and how easy Nate is with the boys." And even more scary how she felt this heightened sense of awareness. "I feel like he's winding himself into our lives." Her foolish thoughts slid back to that moment in the flower shop— the brush of his lips on her forehead and the faint thrill it gave her.

"*Our lives?* As in you and the kids?"

"I can't let this happen. I don't have the reserves—the strength." Mia looked up at her friend, catching the sympathy in her eyes. "He doesn't own a home. He hasn't settled down since he left Denny's parents' ranch. I can't afford to let him take up even the tiniest space in my heart. I have four kids. I have a divorce behind me. My life is a tangle of obligations and trouble and mess and there's no way I can fall for him."

"And yet you have."

"Not all the way," Mia said. "But I'm teetering. And I'm carrying so much baggage that if I tip even a bit more, I will fall. And I don't know where I'll land. And I don't know if I can trust that he'll be around to pick me up. I mean, what man would want to be saddled with four of another man's kids? I feel like I'm making the biggest presumption in the world by even thinking he might be attracted to me."

Evangeline gave her a gentle smile. "I'm not blind. I see the way he looks at you when you're not looking at him. No man looks like that at a woman he's not interested in. I also think Nate is enough of a realist to know what he's getting into by being attracted to you. And I think he genuinely likes your kids."

In spite of her misgivings, Mia's heart fluttered and anticipation sang through her. Had that casual kiss meant what she thought it had? Could she dare think that he wasn't toying with her?

"Nate is a good-looking guy," Evangeline continued. "And he's great with your kids."

"Too great for a single guy," Mia put in, her innate common sense quenching the hope Evangeline's words had created. "It takes nothing and he's making the girls smile, Josh laugh and Nico's eyes sparkle the way they used to." She wrapped her arms around herself in a protective gesture. "Al never even could make the boys laugh the way he does."

"Maybe if Al had a cowboy hat and horses," Evangeline said with a twinkle, her lips pursed as if considering that scenario. Then she grew serious. "I can see what your problem is. But I remember you talking to me when I was so confused about Denny. I had the same issues, only he was the one with the baby. I was afraid and you talked to me about how life isn't always neat and tidy. That sometimes it's messy. And you are right. Falling for Nate right now seems like a mistake. I know from what Denny has told me about him, that Nate had a desperately hard life before he came to the ranch. Maybe he doesn't think he deserves any happiness. But maybe, just maybe, he needs a reason to stay. Maybe he's never had a reason to settle down. Maybe you could give him that reason."

Evangeline's quietly spoken words wound themselves around Mia's lonely and confused heart. But even as the part of her that still longed for her own happy ending, even as the part of her that still hoped romance would come into her life, her reality was her four children. Their happiness and comfort and their needs were first in her life.

She didn't know if she dared open herself up enough to Nate to take a chance that maybe it would work out, maybe it wouldn't.

"Glad to see you boys are wearing your boots," Nate said as he helped Nico into the saddle, and handed him the leather reins. "Now you don't have to worry about your feet slipping through the stirrups."

Nico wiggled his feet as if checking. Then he looked up at Nate and gave him a huge smile.

Things were progressing, thought Nate, his heart quickening at the sight of Nico's happiness.

"I got mine on, too," Josh called out. "I look like a real cowboy now."

Nate gave him a thumbs-up, wishing for a moment he had given in to his impulse and bought the boys each a cowboy hat to boot. Trouble was, he wasn't sure how Mia would have reacted. He didn't know what to think of her not letting the boys wear their new clothes today. Maybe he had insulted her. With someone as proud and independent as she was, you never knew.

He looked over his shoulder to where she sat outside the corrals, blanket spread out on the grass, Grace and Jennifer playing beside her. The sun shone on her short hair, enhancing her delicate, elfinlike features. Her legs in their beige capris were folded up under her. She wore a plain white tank top that left her arms bare to the sun.

She looked great.

She looked up and they exchanged a look that pressed into his heart. His mind skipped easily back to that moment when, once again, he held her in his arms in the burned-out hulk of what was her flower shop. He still wasn't sure what had come over him when he brushed a kiss over her forehead. He would have liked to blame it on sympathy but in his deepest soul he knew it was a different emotion.

"Can I ride my horse by myself?" Josh asked, pulling his attention back to the reason he was here.

"Maybe later," Nate said, walking over to his horse to

fiddle with his stirrups, make sure the cinch was tight. Unnecessary adjustments that gave him a moment to regain his mental equilibrium. "Okay, cowboys, I think we're all set," he said, fitting Josh's foot into the stirrup.

Nate handed Josh the reins. "Don't pull on these. I just want you to get used to the idea of holding them. I'll be leading the horses with the halter ropes."

Josh's drooping lips made him chuckle. "Sad faces won't make me change my mind," he said, giving him a quick grin. "We'll do everything one step at a time."

He untied the halter ropes from the corral fence, clucked to the horses and began the slow circling of the corral just as they had done yesterday. Bella and Nola were, once again, on their best behavior, which surprised him, considering how advanced Nola's pregnancy was. He'd hesitated to use her but also knew that moderate exercise would be good for her.

"You're not taking Tango out?" Denny called out.

Nate glanced back, smiling at his foster brother, who had come out of the house and was now leaning on the fence, his elbows draped over the top rail, ball cap pushed back on his head.

"I took him out this morning. He's still a bit lame, but he's coming along."

"We could bring some cows in if you want. He could work them some."

"Maybe tomorrow."

"Sure. After church would work."

Right. Church. He'd forgotten about that.

"Mommy said we can wear our new clothes to church tomorrow," Josh said. He wiggled in the saddle as if in anticipation. "I'm so excited."

So she had liked the clothes, but was saving them for church. The thought gave him a small thrill of pleasure.

"Okay, boys, today I thought we could ride out in the pasture," Nate said, "so you have to pay attention now."

"Can we gallop?" Josh asked, rocking in his saddle as if getting ready.

"No galloping. You're still learning," Nate said.

"Do you want to go out with the boys?" Nate heard Evangeline ask Mia. "You could lead one of the horses."

Nate glanced back as Evangeline joined Mia on the blanket.

"I could watch the girls," she offered.

Even from here Nate sensed Mia's automatic protest. Her default pushing away of anyone's help. Even after all she'd been through, she still clung to her independence.

"You should go," Denny urged Mia as he tugged her to her feet. "Ella is sleeping and I don't have a lot to do right now. Nate can take you to the river. It's a nice little walk. Give you a chance to get away from the house."

"But I don't have the right shoes." Mia lifted her foot, twisting it to show him the worn sneakers she wore. Probably also from the hand-me-downs she had received for the kids.

"Those will be fine for a walk across the pasture," Nate put in, anticipation singing through him. "Besides, it's a good idea if you come. You can keep an eye on the boys."

Mia looked from her girls to her boys as if trying to decide who needed her more. "All right," she conceded. "But we can't be gone long."

"It's not far," Nate said. "We'll be back soon."

Mia climbed over the corral fence and walked slowly

over to him, running the palms of her hands over her thighs as she gave Nico a quick smile. "You need to know I'm not the bravest person around horses," she said to Nate.

"You don't need to be brave around Nola. She's expecting. You can share pregnancy stories with her."

Mia's laughter made him feel humorous. But her laughter faded when Nate handed her the halter rope. "So what do you want me to do?" she asked.

"Just follow me. I'll lead with Bella."

"Okay."

Nate heard the uncertainty in her voice but knew everything would turn out just fine. He opened the gate of the corral and led Bella out.

They walked slowly through the pasture, side by side, each muted footfall of the horses' hooves leaving the farmyard behind.

"How are you doing?" Nate asked, looking over at Mia.

She gave him a tight smile. "I'm okay. Just never realized how big these animals are." She stumbled as Nola came too close then walked past Mia.

Mia squealed and Nico latched on to the saddle horn, looking suddenly frightened.

"Let's go back," Mia said, fear tingeing her voice.

Nate knew that he had to let Mia overcome this. For Nico's sake as well as Mia's. Also, she needed to put Nola back in her place.

"Make her stop," Nate said, tugging on Nola's halter rope to stop her, embarrassed that Nola had chosen this moment, with this person, to push boundaries.

Mia jumped as Nola crowded her again. "How?"

"She's ahead of you now so pull back on her halter

rope." Thankfully, Nola immediately responded to the pressure. "Now turn and face her straight on. She knows that means she's not going anywhere until you let her."

Mia did and Nola dropped her head, a sign of submission.

"Good. Now you need to make her go backward by putting your hand on her chest and maintaining a steady pressure against it."

"She's way bigger than me. I doubt I can budge her."

"You're not pushing her, just giving her a signal. Just try, but make sure you put full pressure on her chest so she can feel what you're doing."

Mia released a sigh full of doubt, but lifted her hand and did exactly what Nate had told her to. Immediately, Nola took a few steps back.

"Look, Mom, you did it," Josh said, voicing his encouragement of his mother.

"She certainly did," Nate said, winking at Josh. "Your mom is really smart."

"She even knows how to tame monsters," Josh said.

Nate sensed another story behind that comment, judging by Mia's quick glance toward Nico.

"Now release your pressure and pet her on the nose," he said. "Let her know she's done good."

"So that's all it took?" Mia asked as she hesitantly patted Nola. "Just that little push?"

"You weren't pushing her," Nate said. "It's more about pressure and release mixed in with some body language," Nate said, warming to his favorite topic. "Horses are like kids. You need to make it easy for them to do what you want them to and hard for them to do what you don't want them to do."

"I should have taken a course on horse training before I had kids," Mia said, glancing back at Nola as if to make sure she had learned her lesson. Thankfully, Nola stayed where she should. Behind Mia.

"You learn quick," Nate said, giving her a gentle smile.

Her own lips curved in a smile and her brown eyes seemed to turn into amber, her expression stealing his breath.

She was so beautiful.

He wanted to kiss her.

He swallowed down that thought, pulling his head around and facing the path they walked down. This was crazy. She wasn't a woman he could be casual with. He couldn't just date her and then walk away.

But in spite of his self-talk, he found his eyes drawn to the boys silhouetted against the brilliant blue of the sky, and he felt a quieting in his chest. They were good boys and he enjoyed being with them.

A small question raised itself like a delicate plant.

Could he stay? Could he take this on?

"Can we go now?" Josh asked in a plaintive tone. "Nico and I want to see the creek."

"How far away is that?" Mia asked.

He looked at her again, but she was watching Nola, as if making sure she kept her distance.

"It will take a few minutes. I'm sure Evangeline and Denny can manage the girls."

"It's not the girls I'm worried about," she said so quietly Nate wondered if he had heard her properly. Then Mia cocked her head to one side as if listening. "Do you hear that, boys?" she asked.

"The train," Josh called out.

As soon as he spoke, Nate heard the slightly dissonant sound of the train's horn bouncing off the mountains, echoing through the valley.

"How did you hear that so quick?" Nate asked.

"I marked time by that train," Mia said. "It used to pass through town only a few blocks from the flower shop."

The melancholy tone of the train was reflected in her voice and Nate, once again, was hit with how much she had lost. Seeing the burned-down shop yesterday had been difficult for him; he couldn't imagine what it did for her.

"Look, Mommy, your favorite flowers," Josh said, pointing to a clump of pink-and-red plants. "Can I pick some?"

"You'll have to get off the horse," Nate said.

"My mommy loves flowers. I want to get her some."

Nate clucked to the horses to stop and eased Josh off, but Nico just shook his head.

"Don't go too far," Mia warned as Josh ran ahead. He just waved, then bent over and picked some of the flowers he had pointed out.

"Those don't look like flowers to me," Nate said as Josh brought the plants back.

"Technically, they're not flowers. It's called Indian paintbrush," Mia said. "It's the tops of the leaves that turn color. They come in pink and red and shades of orange. But they sure look pretty."

Nate couldn't look away at the gentle smile on Mia's face as she took the flowers from Josh.

"Thanks, buddy."

"I'm going to get more," he said, then ran off toward the trees.

He would return with yet another flower and Mia

would identify them to Nate. Coneflowers, lupins, daisies and shooting stars.

"You know a lot about flowers," he said, full of admiration.

"Occupational hazard," she said, then called out to her son. "Josh, can you get me some of those long grasses and a few more of the purple shooting stars?" she asked.

Josh gladly complied and as he returned, she took the plants he had gathered and with a few deft movements, rearranged them and suddenly, the plants that he would have simply bypassed or ignored, had become a beautiful bouquet.

"Wow. You're really good at that. Did you always like working with flowers?"

Mia shrugged but Nate could see that his compliment pleased her. "I had a huge flower garden at…at the house we used to live in. I loved growing flowers, trying different combinations of colors, textures and shapes." Her voice grew wistful as she turned the bouquet around in her hand, making small adjustments, her smile growing as if working with the flowers brought back good memories.

"Is that why you bought the flower shop?"

Mia's smile faded away. "Partly, but more out of necessity. I had to find a way to support my family after my—" Mia stopped there and glanced back at Nico, but he was looking around, seemingly off in a world of his own. "Anyway, the flower shop was a perfect fit for me," Mia continued. "Living above it meant I could keep my kids close by and still run a business and support my family."

"Do you get support from your ex?" he asked,

switching the halter rope to his other hand. Moving closer to hear her better.

As he did, he caught a faint whiff of lilacs and his hand brushed against hers. He had to stop himself from catching it in his. He knew he should keep his distance but something about her called to him.

Mia's lips pressed together as she twisted a piece of grass around the bouquet. "No. He never calls, never sends the boys anything. I have to fight for every penny of child support." She looked back at Nico again, then lowered her voice, her eyes holding his. "You'd think they would matter. Even just a bit." He easily heard the pain in her voice, understood that these children, who meant so much to her, seemed to mean so little to the man who fathered them. "But the upside of his leaving is that I was pushed to think for myself. And out of that came owning the flower shop."

"So how do you keep yourself busy? Hartley Creek isn't such a big town."

"There's always a birthday or anniversary or wedding that people need flowers for. Larissa at the Morrisey Creek Inn is a steady customer, as are a few other hotel owners. And I sell plants, as well, knickknacks for the house, decorations. It's a steady business. I get a girl to come in and help me when I have an especially busy few days. I'm doing Naomi Deacon's wedding in a couple of weeks and Evangeline's…" Mia's voice faded as if she realized that neither might happen. Then she released a tight laugh. "Anyway, there was lots of business."

And in that moment it seemed the most natural thing in the world to lay his hand on her shoulder. To let his rough fingers lightly slip over her soft skin.

Their steps slowed and it was as if the horses and Josh and Nico's presence retreated, leaving only him and Mia.

She swallowed and then pulled back, looking behind her again at Nico, then over at Josh. As if to remind herself of her own priorities.

Nate swallowed his own confusion, wondering what he was doing. She wasn't some single girl following the rodeo circuit, looking for fun and maybe an evening out. She was more complicated than any girl he had ever dated.

And yet, at the same time, he never felt this settled, this content around any other woman.

Four kids. Four kids.

The words beat at him, but after spending time with her and her family, the thought didn't hold the fear it used to.

"And what about you? How do you put food on the table or hay in the trough, so to speak?" she asked.

Nate let the question hang between them for a beat. "The horses cost more to feed than I do," he said with a light laugh. "But I've managed to keep us all going with my winnings, my earnings at the ranches I work for in the winter and the sale of some horses. I've got two more foals coming up that I hope to sell and a couple of other horses boarded with a friend. Bella and Nola have proven themselves in the cutting horse circuit and have a great pedigree so I'm hoping for good dollars from their offspring."

"I understand that you need to spend a lot of time working with cutting horses," Mia continued. "Don't you need a home base for that?"

"And how do you understand that?" he asked, deflecting her other question.

"I know how to use Google as well as the next person." Her eyes held a twinkle of humor. "And I know that the competition you're heading for is a big one for cutting horses."

"It is. I'm hoping Tango will be strong enough to compete. I've got a lot riding on this."

"And when is Nola supposed to foal?"

"Not for three weeks. I had figured on being in Montana by then. I was going to be managing a ranch there for a friend, a well-known trainer of cutting horses, but my plans might change."

He wasn't sure why he sounded so tentative. Moving to Montana had always been his plan. Staying with Arden Charles and working with him would raise his own profile as a breeder and trainer.

But now?

He gave Mia another glance only to catch her looking at him with a cautious smile as other doubts and possibilities rode into his mind. But they were saddled with a twinge of uncertainty.

He tried to clear them away. He knew he had to stick to his plans. Changing them now was like switching horses midstream.

Every good cowboy knew you didn't do that.

Chapter Nine

"Nico, honey, let me tuck your shirt in." Mia crouched down beside her son on the carpeted floor of the church foyer, letting other people flow past her as she tidied him up. She fingered his hair away from his face and gave him a gentle smile of encouragement, stifling her own disappointment when he didn't return her smile. This morning he had been acting up, sulking and then hiding when it was time to go to church. Mia could see he was frustrated but he wouldn't say anything. Trouble was, she was frustrated, too.

How would Nico react when Nate left?

Mia stood, banishing that thought. For now she clung to the little bit of progress she saw with Nico. She couldn't think further than that. Yet, even as her pragmatic self thought that, the romantic buried beneath loads of laundry, endless cleaning and feeding, clung to every interaction she shared with Nate. Every touch, every look. When Evangeline had mentioned that Nate simply needed a reason to stay, the lonely part of her was tempted by the possibilities.

He's not sticking around for a woman with four

children and you can't allow yourself to entertain that thought.

Much as Mia disliked Other Mother, sometimes she was right.

She caught Nico's and Josh's hands in her own, reminding herself that Al had ditched her because he couldn't imagine being with a mother of four. How could a man who had no biological connection even be remotely interested in taking all that on?

Mia squared her shoulders, firmed her resolve, sent up a prayer for strength and started up the stairs. Then she felt Nico tug her hand and she looked up.

There he stood at the top of the stairs in profile, hair falling across his forehead, mouth quirked in that who-cares smile that she was sure had made the hearts of others flutter, hands tucked into back pockets, his weight shifted on one booted foot. His broad shoulders were enhanced by a white shirt tucked into blue jeans. His features were animated as he spoke. He pulled one hand out of his jeans, his smile growing.

Her heart did an annoying flop in response to seeing him so unexpectedly. She hadn't heard him say he was attending church.

Then, as she took those last few steps up, Nico still tugging on her hand to hurry her along, she discovered the target of Nate's captivating smile.

Young Lacy Miedema stood at the entrance to the sanctuary.

Her sugary-pink dress shimmered in the subdued lighting of the entrance; her blond hair shone and her young smile sparkled. The epitome of all that was young and cute and fun.

Mia glanced at her own dress. It was pretty, but practical. For a moment she wished she had taken Evangeline up on her offer to spruce up her outfit with a scarf or necklace. Then she mentally laughed at herself. As if a scarf or necklace would add enough appeal to offset Lacy, who was young, pretty and free of all liens and encumbrances.

Compared to Mia with her four kids, burned-out business and all the other stuff attached to her like barnacles on a tugboat, Lacy looked like the fairest sailboat in the bay.

She gave Nate a piece of paper that he quickly shoved in his pocket with another smile of thanks.

Then Nico pulled free of her and ran toward Nate, grabbing at his hand.

"Hey, there," Nate said, looking down at Nico. "Good to see you." Then he looked up and his smile deepened.

"Hey, Mia," he said, his deep voice sliding too easily into the empty parts of her life. "Good to see you, too."

In spite of her brave self-talk, Mia was about to return his smile when—

"Wow. Are those the shirts and pants you bought the boys at the store?" Lacy said, grinning up at him. "And how did those dresses fit the girls?"

So that's why he bought the clothes, Mia thought, reality falling like a cold shower. To impress sweet, young Lacy.

"We should go, kids," Mia said. But her boys clung to Nate's hands like barnacles.

"Can you come and sit with us?" Josh asked, swinging Nate's hand.

Nate looked over at Mia, raising his eyebrows as if in question. "That's up to your mom."

Great. If she said no, she would look silly. If she said

yes, she was inviting him into her space. And today, of all days, she needed her time in church. Her time to be nourished and strengthened for the week ahead.

So she simply gave a noncommittal shrug and let Nate interpret that how he willed.

As he followed her, still holding the boys' hands, she guessed he took it as an invitation.

She saw a large enough space beside Renee, her new husband, Zach, and their daughter, Tricia. Renee had sent her a text late last night, telling her that she was back from her honeymoon. Mia hurried down the aisle, eager to catch up with her friend.

Renee looked up as Mia sat down beside her and her features crumpled into an expression of pity.

"Hey, girl," Renee said, slipping her arm around her, giving her a tight hug. "So sorry we couldn't be here for you."

"You were on your honeymoon," Mia said, leaning into her friend's embrace. "I got all your texts."

"So…is it all gone?" Renee asked, pulling back, her hands still resting on Mia's shoulders. "The flower shop? Your house?"

Mia thought of the blackened remnants of her store. Thank goodness she hadn't been able to inspect the apartment above. Seeing that one picture had been hard enough. "It needs some work," she said, trying to sound lighthearted.

"And how is Nico?" Renee asked, lowering her voice to a whisper.

"He's okay physically," was all Mia could say. Her friend's sympathy threatened to draw out fresh sorrow she couldn't allow herself to dwell on. She was only managing by dint of simply putting one foot in front of the other.

Then Renee looked past her as Nate, Josh and Nico settled into the pew beside her.

"Denny's foster brother, Nate Lyster," Mia whispered, answering the question in Renee's eyes.

Nate was too big a complication to explain in the few moments they had left before church started.

Renee gave her an arch look and nodded. "I'll be waiting for more details." Then she frowned as she looked at the dress Mia wore. "Don't remember seeing that before."

Mia glanced down at the simple blue-and-white polka dotted dress she wore. "Larissa Beck came over last night. Brought some clothes for me." While she loved the dress and the other things she'd received, to Mia it was still a reminder of how much she still depended on other people, and on how much she had lost."

"You look cute." Renee tilted her head to one side, her auburn hair sliding over her shoulders. "And I have a feeling this Nate guy agrees with me."

Mia wasn't going to look but it was as if an invisible rope slowly drew her head around and then her eyes met Nate's and it was as if his smile illuminated the lonely places of her life she never thought would see light.

Then the worship team came to the front of the church, picked up their instruments and invited the congregation to join them in song.

Mia rose, thankful for the distraction. Thankful for this moment that she could let music and song bring her to a place of nourishment.

And as she glanced down at Nico between her and Nate, her heart hitched. Nico loved singing, but he stood beside her, leaning forward as if hoping, somehow, to catch the words needed.

Her hope must have shown on her face because, to her surprise, she felt Nate's hand give her shoulder a fleeting squeeze.

But in that transient moment, she felt a connection and support that she had never felt from the man who had fathered her children. She wasn't sure where to put it so she turned her attention back to the song the congregation sang, saving the moment to examine another time.

The worship service flowed on and the familiarity gave Mia a foundation she knew she could stand on. All during the ups and downs of her relationship with Al, her struggles with the life she had compared to the one she had dreamed of, she had clung to God's abiding and constant love. Her shelter and comfort.

After the songs were over, they sat down and Pastor Blacketer came to the front and welcomed everyone.

"And before we go to God in prayer I want to mention how thankful we are that Mia and her family were not hurt in the fire that consumed their building last week." Pastor Blacketer scanned the congregation as if looking for her then made eye contact with her. "We'll be praying for you and for your family as you get through this time." Then he looked around the congregation, pulling them into the moment. "There is a special fund set up for Mia and her family. Contact the deacons if you want to participate."

Mia's spine stiffened at the announcement. Even as she sat straighter, she could feel Renee slip her hand through her arm and bend her head closer. "Just relax. People want to help and it's okay to ask for help."

Mia nodded, tight-lipped. She knew she was being proud but still…

Her neck warmed, then tingled and again she found herself looking over at Nate, who gave her a faint wink and a smile. As if he understood. She returned the smile, suddenly thankful for his presence. Then, Nico yawned and to her utter surprise, leaned over and laid his head on Nate's lap. She wanted to catch him, pull her against her side.

But Nate didn't move. Didn't object. Instead, he lifted his hand and carefully brushed Nico's hair back from his forehead, then rested his hand on Nico's shoulder, as if anchoring him.

Mia couldn't look away from the sight, her heart both full and weightless with a peculiar emotion. Then Nate looked over at her and their gazes meshed and held and it was as if her being, so long dry and empty, was slowly being nourished and filled by this man.

You can't let this happen. Not with this man.

But even as Other Mother chided her and made her turn her head back to the pastor, the lonely portion of her soul was fully aware of Nate during the rest of the service.

He was looking forward to the day.

Nate splashed water on his face, toweled off then gave his reflection in the mirror a quick grin. It had been a while since he was excited about what the day would bring. Part of the reason for his excitement was Tango's progress. Today, he wanted to put Josh on him.

The other was the thought of spending time with Mia and the kids again.

For the past couple of weeks his life had fallen into a rhythm that, surprisingly, created a sense of grounding.

Each morning this past week, Mia brought the boys out to the corral for them to ride the horses. Mostly, she and the girls would sit on a blanket by the corrals and when they got fussy, she would bring them inside for a nap.

When he was done with the boys, he brought them to the house. Each time he did he meant to drop them off and then leave. But each time he got to the house he found himself lingering. Tuesday, Mia had just made cookies and asked if he wanted some and wouldn't lemonade go well with them?

Each day he would stay longer, talk more. They discovered a joint love of mystery novels and biographies. They had read many of the same authors.

Josh and Nico would hang around for a while and then go play. Nico was still locked in his silence but he always had a special smile for Nate.

But each time Nate left the house, it was with a curious reluctance. And a growing attraction to Mia and her quiet strength in the face of everything she lost.

Each evening, however, after spending the afternoons cutting hay and fixing fences for Denny on the ranch, he would head to town for dinner in spite of Evangeline's objections. For a reason he couldn't entirely explain himself, he wanted to keep his time with Mia and her children separate from Denny and Evangeline. He wasn't sure himself what was happening, but he did know that for the first time in years, he felt a quieting of the restlessness that had been his constant companion since leaving the Norquest ranch.

He stepped out of the trailer and strode across the

yard, the cool of the morning a harbinger of the fall that hovered around the corner.

As he caught Tango, his mind slipped to the futurity and beyond. The ranch he was supposed to be working at in a month. Getting the job there had been like a dream come true.

But now?

He brushed the questions aside as he saddled up Tango, running his hands down his legs, sending up a quick prayer of thanks for Tango's healing.

"Another week and you'll be ready, I think," Nate said as he buckled the bridle on.

He felt the usual clench of tension when he thought of the futurity and what was, literally, riding on it. Everything he had done, every decision he had made, had been working toward it. It was going to be his way of proving that Karl was wrong.

Then he heard the excited chatter of Josh's voice and he turned in time to see Nico and Josh clambering up the fence. They were good listeners, though, and as he had taught them, didn't come into the corral until Nate told them they could.

Mia was behind them but she was alone.

"Where're the girls?"

"Evangeline is home today," Mia said. "She offered to babysit and I accepted."

"Wow. Letting people help you," Nate said, unable to keep the faint teasing note out of his voice.

"I let people help me," she protested as she crouched down to pet Socks.

"Not very often," he said, thinking of the many times this week he had offered to carry the girls into the house and her steady insistence that no, she was fine.

She shrugged as she flicked her hands through her hair. He caught the glint of gold hoops dangling from her ears. She looked brighter today. More cheerful.

And as he looked at her more closely he realized what was different. Instead of her T-shirt and pants that she usually wore, today she wore a light blue shirt with a white skirt that flowed around her knees. She also looked as if she was wearing makeup.

If it was possible, she looked even prettier than she did before. More feminine.

"So why are you using Tango?" Mia asked.

He pulled his attention back to his horse as he let the final stirrup fall. "Nola is kind of cranky. I'm afraid she might be foaling sooner than I thought. I put her in the barn just to be on the safe side." Nate thought of the extra complication this situation could create for him.

"I really, really want to see a baby horse," Josh said, his voice taking on a dreamy tone. "That would be so cool."

"If she foals, you'll see one," Nate said.

"Promise?" Josh leaned ahead, his eyes gleaming with anticipation. Beside him, Nico almost quivered with excitement, holding out his hand in entreaty. As if he was making his own silent request.

Nate looked from Mia to Josh to Nico, then nodded. "Sure. Of course you can see it." He turned back to Josh. "So, buddy, let's get you mounted up."

"Will Josh be okay?" Mia asked. "Tango's bigger than Nola."

He glanced back and caught the flash of worry in Mia's face. "He's a good horse," he assured her. "Completely bomb proof."

"And you would know this how?" she asked with a hint of humor.

Nate returned her smile. "Means nothing will scare or startle him. I wouldn't put Josh on Tango if I didn't trust him completely." Nate's smile deepened. "I hope you trust me."

Mia held his gaze a beat longer then looked up at her boys, perched on the top of the corral fence, silhouetted against a glorious blue sky. "I'm trusting you with what is most important to me."

Her words created a consolation that he didn't realize he needed until she spoke. "That means a lot to me."

Then before he could reveal too much more of himself, he looped the reins around the saddle, caught Tango by the halter rope and brought him to Josh. He helped the boy on, got him settled and then handed him the reins. "Remember what I showed you last week?" he said to Josh. "How I showed you how to steer a horse?"

Josh nodded, his eyes sparkling with anticipation. Nate gave Tango another quick once-over but Tango stood quietly, his one foot cocked, his weight shifted over his other three feet. The epitome of relaxation and trust.

"Today, I thought you could try yourself," Nate said, looping the halter rope over the saddle.

"Are we going into the pasture again?" Josh asked.

Nate shook his head. "For now you need to learn how to handle Tango in the corral." He walked beside Josh a couple of rounds, making him turn left and right and then when he was satisfied Josh had it figured, he called to Nico.

Nico jumped off the fence and ran over, his booted feet creating small puffs of dust, his eyes bright with

anticipation, Mia close behind him. As Nate lifted him
into the saddle, Nico caught the reins in his hands, an
expectant look on his face as Nate untied the halter rope
from the hitching rail.

Not too hard to guess what he wanted.

"Sorry, buddy," Nate said. "Your mom will lead you
around while I keep an eye on Josh."

Nico looked from Nate to his mother, opened his
mouth and something like a groan escaped.

Nate's heart thudded in his chest at the faint sound.
This was the first time since he started working with
Nico that anything close to a sound had escaped his lips.

Mia stared up at him, one hand holding the halter
rope, the other pressed over her chest, as if to hold her
heart in.

Nico breathed heavily in and out, as if trying to say
more but nothing more came out. He slouched in the
saddle, a doleful expression on his face. Mia placed her
hand on his back, stroking it gently as if coaxing something else out of him.

"Were you trying to tell us something, buddy?" Nate
encouraged.

Nico's expression was one of entreaty. Nate wished
he could get inside the boy's head and figure out what
was holding him back from talking. Instead, he patted him on the leg and gave him a quick smile. "You're
doing great, little guy. You're a real cowboy, you know
that? And because you're so good on the horse, I want
you to keep an eye on your mother while she walks
beside you."

Nico nodded as a slow smile curved his lips and
then Nico caught Nate's hand and clung to it, squeez-

ing hard. As he did, Nate felt something unfurl in him. Some elemental connection between him and this kid.

Is this what it felt like to be a father?

And right behind his question came the pastor's words of yesterday.

"Forget the former things..." It sounded too easy, but at the same time the words had resonated with him. Bringing back the lessons he'd learned at the Norquests'.

He wasn't in this business of life alone.

He allowed tenuous feelings that had vibrated between them all week to settle into his soul. He let a tentative vision slip into his mind. Him and Mia. And her kids. A family.

Her hand had drifted down from Nico's back and rested on the saddle. It only took a little movement, a barely discernible shift and his hand was over hers, squeezing lightly.

Her lips parted and her breath quickened. He swallowed, feeling as if he teetered on the edge of something large. Important.

Fragments of thoughts and emotions whirled through his head. She was everything he had ever hoped to find in a woman.

She comes with four kids.

You're not in this alone.

Nate drew a deep, cleansing breath as questions and expectations shimmered between them. Could he truly be what she needed?

You're not in this alone.

He felt his breath catch in his throat as the distance between them lessened. As the kids, the horses and everything around them faded into a distant echo and there was only him and Mia. His hand came up to touch her cheek, their breaths seemed to mingle.

You are useless.

The angry voice from the deeper past slammed into him with all the force of his stepfather's fists. Nate blinked as if waking up from a sleep, his hand dropping suddenly to his side.

Nobody wants you, not even your mother. Should have gotten rid of you when I had the chance. You're useless.

Nate tore his gaze away from Mia, frustrated that his stepfather and his vitriol haunted him still. Surely he had outgrown his stepfather's poisonous words.

"My reins are tangled," Josh called out.

Nate pulled away, thankful for the distraction. As he walked back to Josh he forced himself back into the present, stifling past memories of the stings of the slaps, the pain of the fists. The countless humiliations he'd endured at his stepfather's hands.

You can't be what she needs, was the final voice that resonated as he sorted Josh's reins. *You don't have the ability.* The words beat through his head in time to the quiet thuds of the horse's hooves.

And yet, as he walked around the corral, his eyes kept seeking and finding Mia. And as he watched her patient actions with Nico, heard her quiet reassurances to her son, other questions braided themselves through the other voices resonating through his mind.

Could I do this?

Do I dare?

Chapter Ten

"Are you going to read to us?" Josh asked, handing Mia the books he had chosen from the cardboard box beside their bed.

Mia blinked, pulling herself back to the present and her sons. She had just put the girls to bed, but as she had come into the boys' room, her mind had done what it had all afternoon. Slipped back to that moment in the corral; that almost moment when she and Nate faced each other, questions hovering between them.

"Yes, of course I am," she said with a quick smile, taking the books Josh and Nico gave her.

She settled herself on the bed between them and opened the book. But as her lips read the words, her traitorous mind wandered, once again, back to Nate.

All through the week, with each conversation they shared, each moment they spent together, she sensed a growing awareness.

She wasn't sure if her heightened feelings for Nate were a result of feeling vulnerable after seeing Nico struggle to speak and losing her house and business, or if it was because something real was growing between her and Nate.

She just knew that each day she spent around him, her own feelings were shifting and changing.

Don't be foolish. What would a single, good-looking man like him see in you?

Mia fought down the frustration Other Mother's words created in her. She knew they were true, but oh, for that one moment when it seemed attraction trembled between her and Nate, she felt appealing.

"Mommy, you stopped reading," Josh said, patting her hand.

"Sorry, buddy. My mind was wandering."

Wandering to places you shouldn't be going.

Mia sighed as she picked up the book again. Other Mother was annoying, but at times she was right. Mia had no room for romance in her life. Not with four children and a business she needed to get back off the ground.

She closed the book she had just finished reading as a sudden heaviness weighed down on her. *Please Lord, help me through this,* she prayed as she opened the second book. *Help me to know that I am not doing this on my own. To draw on Your strength to focus on what I need to do. Not some foolish notion of romance and love.*

But even as she said the prayer, regret plucked at her thoughts. If only…

She brushed that aside as she bent over and brushed a kiss over her sons' heads. Then she picked up the book again. But just as she began reading she heard muffled voices coming from downstairs, raised in excitement.

Then the sound of feet coming up the stairs and a hesitant knock on the door.

"Come in," Mia said, puzzled as to what was happening.

The door creaked open and Nate put his head through the opening. "Do you want to see Nola's foal? It was just born."

He addressed them all, but his eyes held hers.

"Yippee," Josh called out, scrambling off the bed. Then he grabbed Mia's hand, pulling. "Can we go see? Please?"

Nico picked up on the excitement and was yanking on Mia's other hand.

Mia caught their enthusiasm, her own excitement also growing. "Yes, you can. We need to get your jackets, though."

Then she looked at Nate. "It will be okay, won't it?"

"She's in a pen. It will be fine."

Then he smiled at her, his eyes crinkling at the corners with a hint of suppressed humor. And when she returned his smile she felt, once again, that sense of waiting.

A few minutes later, Mia, Josh and Nico joined Evangeline and Denny. They stood quietly in the barn, the light at the end of the barn casting a soft glow over the pen. Right beside Nola lay a small, perfectly formed foal, shaking its head as if trying to figure out what just happened. Nola lay on her side, as if still recuperating from the ordeal. Mia could easily identify with the poor mare. Nola lifted her head, looking over at them as if asking for privacy. Then she slowly struggled to her feet.

Nico sat quietly, intent on the helpless creature lying

on the straw still wet from the birth, legs still folded under itself. Mia looked from the foal to her son, who was almost vibrating. What was going through his mind?

The foal looked around, then its feet pawed at the straw as it struggled to get up.

"Relax, baby," Mia whispered. "Take a breath."

The foal got its feet under it, then fell again. One more time it tried but it couldn't get up.

"Do you need to help it?" Mia asked, tension rising up inside her. If it didn't get up, it probably couldn't drink.

"No. It has to do it on its own." Nate sounded calm, so Mia took her cue from him and made herself relax.

Finally, Nola rose up, her legs shaking with her previous exertions. She took a few halting steps closer to her foal, nudging it with her nose. Then she began licking it.

"Why is Nola doing that?" Josh whispered.

"The licking helps clean the foal off and helps its blood get moving." Nate watched a moment longer, then set Nico down on the ground. "I want to get Nola some water," Nate said.

Nico climbed up, hanging over the edge, watching. Mia smiled at his rapt expression.

Nate returned a few moments later with a pail of water and brought it inside the pen.

"Hey, girl, you did good," Nate said to his horse, his voice low and quiet as he crouched down. "You got yourself a little baby."

"Can you tell what it is?" Denny asked.

"I need a closer look, but I want to give Nola space. Mares are always unpredictable after a birth."

Mia could identify. She remembered the waves of

sorrow mingled with anger that washed over her after the twins were born. Two other women gave birth that day and they had husbands with them, whereas her own husband had been gone. Thankfully Renee had come with her and been by her side but it wasn't the same as having a husband present. The father of the children.

Quiet descended again and Nola continued her licking. Every now and then the colt would try to get up and fall again.

After a few minutes Nate got up and took a tentative step toward the foal. Mia was surprised to see the worry on her son's face.

Then Mia looked in time to see Nola's ears flattened against her head. One hoof flashed out so fast it was back on the floor of the pen before Mia realized what had happened.

Then before anyone could stop him, Nico jumped into the pen, running straight toward Nate, his face a mask of fear.

Nola took one stiff-legged step toward Nico but Nate looped an arm around the boy and yanked him back.

That's twice Nate has saved my son, Mia thought to herself. She sagged against the pen, her legs suddenly two pieces of boneless rubber. Her heart slowed, as she caught her breath.

Then Nico pointed to Nola and grunted again.

"She'll settle down soon," Nate was saying, his arms wrapped around the little boy. "Don't worry. I won't go close to her again."

Nico groaned once more, the guttural sound tearing at Mia's heart but at the same time creating a spark of hope. Then she felt Evangeline's arm around her shoulder. "It's a start," Evangeline said, voicing Mia's own thoughts.

Mia blinked, frustrated at the tears that prickled her eyelids. Too many emotions. Too much to deal with, she told herself.

Then finally the foal staggered to its feet. It rocked a few moments, but seemed to catch its balance. Nola nickered quietly, the motherly sound a complete reversal of her behavior of a few minutes ago. The foal tottered toward her, its hooves rustling in the straw as it bumped into Nola's side.

Then, finally, it started to drink. They all watched a few moments, and then Mia caught Josh yawning. "Hey, buddy, you need to get to bed," Mia said. "It's been a long day for you."

To her surprise Josh didn't protest. Instead, he simply climbed down off the pen. "Is Nico coming?"

"Just give me a minute," Mia heard Nate say.

"We'll take you back to the house, buddy," Denny said.

"It's okay—" Mia was about to say when she caught Evangeline's reprimanding look. She thought of Nate's sardonic comment that she didn't often accept help.

So she relaxed her shoulders then smiled at Denny. "Thanks so much," she said. "I'll be by as soon as Nico can come out."

After they left, Mia moved closer to where Nate and Nico still sat, hooking her arms over the rough wood of the pen, glancing from Nate still holding Nico to Nola who now stood quietly nursing her foal.

"See how the foal is drinking," Nate whispered to Nico. "See how quiet Nola is. She'll be even better in an hour."

Then after a few moments Nate slowly stood, carefully turned and set Nico on the other side of the pen in the aisle of the barn. He looked down at him, ruffling his hair, his expression inscrutable.

"I didn't think Nola would react like that," he said, giving Mia a rueful look. "I'm so sorry."

"Not your fault," Mia said, still shaky after the fact. "I still don't know why Nico jumped into the pen."

Nate shrugged, then gave her a careful smile as if he was unsure of her reaction. "I have a feeling he thought Nola was going to do something to me. Is that right, Nico?"

Nico, who had been pushing some straw around with the toe of his cowboy boot, looked up at Nate, then, to Mia's shock and surprise, nodded.

Nate swung his legs over the partition, then crouched down in front of Nico. "I was being careful, buddy. I wouldn't have let her hurt me."

Nico looked up at Nate, his expression one of complete adoration. Then he launched himself at Nate again, clinging to him. But this time he made no sound.

"Hey, buddy, hope you have good dreams," Nate said, returning Nico's hug. Then he ruffled his hair and gently pulled away.

Mia caught Nico's hand and looked over at the foal and its mother, feeling a connection to her. Then her eyes slipped to Nate and the feeling gained strength and intensity.

Feelings so strong they were almost tangible hummed between them. And when Mia turned to bring Nico back to the house, she knew she would be back.

Nate watched from inside the pen as the foal went down again after nursing from Nola. If he didn't imprint on the foal within the next few hours, it would be too late. Thankfully, Nola had settled down and was more accepting of his presence. He pulled the towel he'd had ready and walked over to the foal, kneeling toward the back of it and grasping its muzzle. He gently flexed it back to the withers to control it and prevent it from standing then started toweling the foal dry.

He heard a whine from the other side of the pen then a rustle as Socks settled himself.

"It's okay, Socks," he reassured his dog. "I got this under control."

As he worked, patiently wiping the foal, preventing it from standing, he kept one watchful eye on Nola, but she showed no more signs of aggression, seemingly content to watch.

"And you're a little colt," Nate said as he worked his way up the animal's body. "Good, I was hoping for another male to work with. You come from some nice bloodlines. You're going to be a goer, like Tango. I just hope we can get to that futurity on time. Though I wonder…" He let his voice trail off as new uncertainties dogged him.

On his way back from town this afternoon he had gotten a phone call from the lawyer handling his stepfather's estate.

Nate still wasn't sure what to do, what to think anymore, so he had given him a noncommittal response. A change from the flat-out no he had given him a couple of weeks ago.

Coming to the ranch, meeting Mia, connecting with her kids… All that had created a drifting of his thoughts to places he had never dared contemplate. A woman he

was attracted to. A woman who made him think of settling. Of changing his rootless, wandering ways.

But even as he let that idea slip through his mind,
right behind it came the uncertainty. The fear.

The biggest lesson Nate had learned in life was letting people get close only meant heartache when they
either left or they hurt you. His mother, his stepfather.
The Norquests. The ranch he thought had become his
refuge. Too many losses meant too much pain.

Much easier to stay alone. Keep your heart guarded
and safe.

He continued his rhythmic stroking of the colt. This
newborn animal not only had a mother to watch over
him, he also had Nate.

And who had been watching out for him?

He heard the muted rolling of the heavy barn door
and he looked up. A gentle warmth coursed through
him when Mia stopped by the gate to the pen, her hands
resting on the top gate, a question in her brown eyes.

"What are you doing?" she asked.

"Imprinting," he said as Nola nickered at the colt that
struggled against Nate again. This time he released it
as it scrambled over to Nola's side and began drinking again. "It's a first, critical step in training horses."

"Did you do that with your other horses?" Mia asked.

He nodded. "The last foal I imprinted on was Tango."

And that had happened in a drafty, broken-down
barn on a ranch he'd been managing for someone else.
This ranch wasn't his place, but after spending a week
and a half here it felt more like home.

Melancholy tunneled through him. It had been a long
time since he felt at home. Not since he lived with the

Norquests. Not since he and Denny worked together on the ranch.

I could get my own place. Use Karl's money.

The thought created a bitter taste on his tongue and yet, as he looked down at Mia, his perspective shifted.

"So Nico settled down okay?" Nate asked, leaning against the gate.

Mia pressed her lips together and then sat down on the hay bale behind her, her hands twisting around each other. "You heard him, didn't you?"

Nate knew precisely what she was talking about and nodded, his own heart thudding at the memory.

"I wish I knew what it meant…." Her voice trailed off as she looked up at him, her eyes holding a shadow of pain. "It seemed to me that he was trying to warn you."

Nate ran his thumb along the rough wood of the pen, her words dipping into his heart, stirring some elemental emotion. "That's what I thought, too."

He looked over at her as words hovered on the edges of his mind. Words that would articulate the flurry of emotions he felt around her and her kids.

"You look scared," she said with a nervous laugh.

He couldn't admit it yet. The time with his stepfather had taught him not to show fear. Not to let anyone see.

But something must have registered with Mia because she gave him a knowing look.

"What are you scared of?" she asked, her voice quiet, gently probing.

There it was. The question that, if answered honestly, would voice the very things he had spent the past few years running and hiding from.

His innate sense of self-preservation kicked in and

he answered her question with a question. "Why do you want to know?"

She pressed her thumbs together as she seemed to consider his query. She swallowed and drew in a quivering breath. "This isn't easy for me, either, you know."

Her oblique comment gave him pause. But as it settled in, he realized what steps she was taking in the hesitant dance that was a relationship between a man and a woman. The dance they had been indulging in all week.

Then he looked at Mia and it was as if the weariness of his relentless, restless wandering finally came to rest like a burden on his shoulders.

He pushed himself away from the pen and came to sit beside her. He held her eyes, drawing strength from her. And, in the back of his mind, a small prayer formed.

Help me, Lord. You promised me I wasn't alone. Help me now.

"You know I was a foster child?"

"Denny told me you came to the ranch when you were about twelve. You lived with your stepfather? Was he the reason you ended up in care?"

"Karl was the type of man who treated his horses far better than he ever treated me." Nate couldn't keep the bitter note out of his voice, which frustrated him. He had tried, over time, to scrub away any memories of Karl. He didn't want Karl to own any part of his mind.

"Did he own a ranch, as well?"

Nate nodded, his mind ticking back to the letter from the lawyer and the opportunities Karl's legacy presented. The money could give him a start. A down payment on a new life.

In spite of that, his gut twisted at the thought of

taking anything from a man who had taken so much from him.

"He trained cutting horses," Nate said. "He was a top-notch trainer. Well-known. I learned a few things from him, good and bad."

Mia was quiet a moment. "Can I ask why you were put into foster care?"

Nate leaned forward, clasping his hands together, trying not to delve too deeply into the past and yet tell her enough to explain. "Karl was a good horse trainer, but didn't know how to handle kids. He was rough and nasty and unforgiving. Eventually, there were a few too many reports from a neighbor, plus a few too many visits to the hospital by me. Karl could blame only so many broken bones on horse accidents." He stopped there, aware that he was veering close to self-pity territory.

He felt Mia's hand rest lightly on his forearm, as if anchoring him. "I'm so sorry," she said quietly. "I didn't realize that. What a horrible thing to deal with, to remember...." Her voice trailed off.

He gave her a careful smile. "I try not to let the memories take over."

Mia's features softened with pity. That bothered him more than he cared to admit.

"You don't have to feel sorry for me," he said. "I'm not a victim. I'm in charge of my life. I go where I want and do what I want."

Mia's smile stiffened and he realized how his bluster sounded. "Denny said something about it being ironic that you raise and train cutting horses," she said. "Is that because of your stepfather?"

Nate let the question settle a moment, going back to the times his stepfather had told him he would never make a trainer—that he was hopeless and a waste of skin.

"Have you ever watched cutting horses work?" he asked, deflecting her question.

"Never even heard of them until you came rolling into town," she said, seemingly willing to go along with his conversational switch.

"Limping more like," he said. He leaned back against the barn wall, stretched his legs out as if getting comfortable. But looking over at Mia, catching her profile in the subdued light of the barn, he realized that he truly was. Comfortable. He couldn't remember the last time he had felt this relaxed around anyone.

"So tell me about working a cutting horse," Mia urged.

"When you're working with a cutting horse in competition, the rider doesn't control the reins," Nate said, crossing his arms over his chest. "He sits in a position that is called Cutter's Slump—leaning back but with shoulders forward and hands on the pommel of the saddle. You use your feet to move the horse, but you don't control it with your hands as it moves and sweeps. I depend on the horse to know what it's doing as much as he or she depends on me to give it just enough guidance to do the job properly."

"Seems like it's more about partnership," Mia said, perfectly articulating what he had tried to say.

"Exactly."

"But don't you need to be around cattle to train cutting horses?" she asked.

"I go on the road with them for competitions, but on the off-season I usually manage a ranch for the winter, like the one I'm headed to after the competition."

Mia nodded, braiding her fingers together. "And that way you're not tied down?"

Nate heard the underlying tone in her question. Guessed where she was going with it. He took a chance and caught one of her hands in his, running his fingers over her blunt fingernails.

"I used to think that I had to be in charge of my life," he said, his voice quiet. "Move when I wanted. A restless, windblown wandering. I feel like I was looking for something I couldn't put my finger on. I always thought I would recognize it when I found it. But lately…" He let the sentence trail off, old fears and worries rising up as if warning him not to let Mia close. Not to take this final step.

"Lately…" Mia encouraged, her voice breathless.

Nate threaded his fingers through hers, looked into her eyes and took a chance. "Lately, I feel like everything that was important to me is shifting and changing. I've lost my footing."

"I feel like I've never had my footing," Mia returned with a shaky laugh.

Nate heard the insecurity in her voice, puzzled as to how she could think that. "You're an amazing person," he said, struggling to find the words to reassure her. "You're an amazing mother. The patience you show with your kids, the love."

"That's not amazing," she said with a dismissive wave of her hand. "That's just being a mother."

"Not every mother is like that," he said quietly.

Mia looked over at him. "Maybe not, but many are."

"I can't imagine many mothers who have had to deal with the stuff you have—raising four kids on your own, losing your business—and still be a patient and loving mother."

She was quiet at that, as if she wasn't sure how to refute him.

"But you're more than that," he said, unable to stop himself. "You are a caring person. Generous and giving." He took her face in his hand, gently stroking his thumb over her delicate chin. "You're beautiful…." His words faded away as her eyes grew wide with surprise and amazement.

"You look like you don't believe me," he said with a light laugh.

"I don't feel very beautiful."

Nate stroked her face as if imprinting her features into his mind. Her breath quickened and he felt a release of resistance. He moved closer, waiting, measuring.

"You may as well know, I want to kiss you," was all he could say.

She opened her mouth as if to say something, then, to his surprise, she reached out and cupped his chin in her hand, as if giving him permission.

Nate closed the small gap between them and, giving in to the attraction that quivered between them, he brushed his lips lightly over hers. A gentle touch. She leaned closer and as they shared a slow, gentle kiss, a voice in the back of his mind warned him.

But for now he stifled it. For now he was with Mia, and that was as far as he wanted to think.

Chapter Eleven

Mia's heart trembled in her chest as she reluctantly drew back from Nate's kiss.

Had this handsome, wonderful man really kissed her? Mia VerBeek? Mother of four?

She hardly dared believe it happened and yet, as she looked into his eyes she saw the light in them and dared to believe that what was happening between them was real. Was true.

"You are beautiful," he repeated, his hands lingering on her face, sending shivers chasing each other down her spine. "It was the first thing I noticed about you."

"That and the twins," she said with a light laugh, injecting a note of reality into a distinctly unreal situation.

"Them, too."

In the pen beyond she saw Nola looking down. Probably inspecting her new baby like any mother would. Mia ran her hands over her legs, trying to find a way to voice her misgivings.

"You seemed uncomfortable when you found out they belonged to me." She spoke quietly, hesitant to relive that moment, yet feeling as if it was necessary to discuss.

Nate leaned forward and Socks got up and padded over to him. Nate stroked his ears, frowning lightly. "When I first saw you I was attracted to you. I thought you were single. I'm not going to lie, it had been a while since I saw someone as pretty as you."

"Oh, c'mon," she said, waving her hand as if dismissing his comments.

"Think what you want. That was my initial reaction," Nate said. "I wanted to get to know you better. Then I saw the babies and I thought, of course. The best ones are always taken."

"So it wasn't the kids that put you off?"

"No. You didn't give me much of a chance to say different." He gave Socks a final pet. "When I found out you had four kids, it…changed things for me—"

"Of course it did," she cut in.

"Hey. I want to be honest with you. Just give me a chance here," Nate said, catching her hands in his again.

"Sorry."

"I told you how I grew up. I never thought I had the necessary skills or background to take on the responsibility of being a father."

Mia was surprised at his admission. "But you're so good with my kids."

"I like them," he said. "They scare me, but I like them."

"They scare me, too," Mia said with a laugh. "Sometimes I walk around the house wondering who these kids are and why they are calling me 'Mom.' Then I realize, they're mine." She grew serious. "I'm glad you like my kids. Anything that happens to me, happens to them."

"I know," he said. Then he sighed. "You don't have to tell me if you don't want, but I'm curious about Al. Your ex-husband. What happened?"

Mia bit her lip, not sure herself she wanted to revisit that place.

"Al and I had a rocky marriage from the start. He liked to go out and party and I liked to stay home. He didn't want kids and I wanted a huge family. We compromised on the two boys." Her mind ticked back to the incendiary argument they'd had when he found out she was pregnant with Nico. She always wondered if her son had heard that from the shelter of the womb. If it had imprinted on his mind somehow. "Anyhow, we stumbled along. I had made a promise and I keep my promises." She shrugged, as if apologizing for that tendency.

Nate gave her shoulder a squeeze. "That's a good thing, you know."

She gave him a quick smile, then returned to her story. "Though things were falling apart, I got pregnant again with the girls. Al accused me of manipulation, which was a joke. It wasn't like we spent a lot of time together at this point in our marriage. Then he told me that I had two choices. I could either terminate the pregnancy and stay married to him, or keep the babies and be a single mother." She pressed her lips against the anger that could still rise up in her at Al's matter-of-fact appraisal of the situation. How calm he had been.

Nate's fingers dug into her shoulder. "Why do some people treat life, people, kids, so carelessly?"

She heard the underlying anger in his voice.

"I don't know," she continued, "but needless to say, I

didn't choose him. And he didn't choose me." She spoke the words easily, even though they cost her much. She always knew for her there was no choice, but for her husband to so effortlessly cast them off could still jar.

Nate sat up and turned her to face him. "He was and is a fool." The anger in his voice was a consolation and an affirmation of who she was. She gave him a tentative smile, still unsure of what had transpired between them. Still hesitant to anchor it too deeply in her life.

Mia leaned against him, the silence of the barn broken only by the faint rustling coming from the pen. She wondered what Nate was going to do about his horses. About the futurity he had been headed for before his plans got derailed.

The mother part of her wanted to ask him about his plans and his intentions.

The woman part of her, the part that enjoyed being with this single, attractive man, kept the questions at bay. For now, this was enough.

"I think you might be okay in time for the competition." Nate clucked to Tango and he stepped up the pace, trotting across the pasture toward the ranch yard. Tango moved smoothly, not much trace of the limp he'd been struggling with. He'd worked with Tango all day Saturday and Sunday, pleased at the horse's progress. It had been almost two weeks since the accident and every day the futurity came closer. He was supposed to be finishing Tango's training at Arden's ranch.

If you're still going.

The question threaded through him, creating second thoughts. Did he have to leave? Couldn't he stay here and work Tango on Denny's ranch?

But he would be making money managing the other ranch. Money he needed to keep his horses fed and himself fed until he got himself established. Even more important, he would be making valuable connections that he could use to start his own business. Set up his own place.

But all this would take time.

You could use Karl's money.

His hands tightened on the reins as anger and loathing coiled through him. Taking Karl's money would be like proving that he needed a man he swore would never have any part of his life.

But you're moving in a different direction. You kissed Mia a couple of days ago. You didn't do that lightly.

He shook off the voices roiling in his head. He didn't dare look too far ahead. For now, he knew that Mia was becoming important to him.

Can you do this? Can you be the man she needs?

He wanted to be. Women like Mia didn't come around often in a person's life.

Thinking of her four children in the abstract scared him. But when he thought of the kids individually—Josh, Nico, Jennifer and Grace—that didn't create the same sense of panic.

On Sunday, after church, they had taken a walk through town. Nate had treated the kids to ice cream and they had gone to the park. It had been one of those days you see on commercials for minivans or life insurance.

The perfect family. Something he'd been looking for most of his life. He'd had a taste of it with the Norquests.

And look what happened there.

Nate pushed the fleeting thought aside. He knew that

he'd let his losses seep too deeply into his life and affect his decisions. Constantly being on the move kept him from putting down roots that could be pulled up. And each uprooting hurt.

Forget the former things. Do not dwell on the past. See I am doing a new thing. Now it springs up. Do you not perceive it?

Right behind those words from Isaiah came thoughts of Mia. Her tenderness and her love for her kids. The way her smile lit up her face when she looked at him. How she seemed so genuine.

Forget the former things.

Nate drew in a deep, cleansing breath, then as he dismounted, he looked over at the house. Evangeline and Denny's vehicles were gone. Mia's was still there. His timing was perfect.

He unsaddled Tango, checked on Nola, then, knowing he couldn't put it off anymore, he took a steadying breath and stepped out of the barn into the welcoming morning air.

As he walked toward the house, his heartbeat quickened in anticipation.

He opened the porch door and when he stepped inside was immediately assaulted by the muffled wailing of babies and Josh sobbing. "I'm sorry, Mommy. I didn't mean to," was all he could hear.

What was going on?

Through all this he caught the faint murmurs of Mia's consoling voice. "It's okay, honey. Don't worry. Mommy's not angry with you," she was saying.

He stopped at the sink to wash and dry his hands, then followed the cacophony and unpleasant odor to the bathroom down the hall from the kitchen. Just inside the door he saw Jennifer clinging to the cabinet door, mouth wide open, tears streaming down her cheek. Grace was also crying and trying to pull herself up on Mia, who was crouched beside the toilet, her arm around Josh. The boy was bent over it, crying, as well. Nico huddled in the bathtub, arms clasped over his head as if to shut out the intense noise.

"I don't want to be sick. I hate being sick," Josh was wailing, clinging to either side of the toilet.

"Sweetie, it will all be over soon." Mia's voice was barely audible over the shrieking.

The entire scene was chaos and Nate never felt more helpless. But he couldn't stand there and do nothing.

Jennifer, still crying, lowered herself to all fours and crawled toward the door. Grace, still wailing as well, followed.

"Jennifer, come back here," Mia called out above the noise, still holding Josh. "Grace, stay here." She caught the second baby just as Josh started crying again.

Nate grabbed the wayward twin heading past him around her middle and heaved her off the ground. Mia looked up and when she saw him her shoulders sagged in relief.

"Cavalry is here," he said as Mia tried to corral Grace. "What can I do?"

Mia bit her lip, her gaze shooting from Josh to Grace, who was wiggling free from her clutches. "Josh is sick and I'm supposed to go to Cranbrook with Nico later this morning."

"I know," Nate said. He had heard from Evangeline.

Then Grace escaped her clutches, heading toward Nate and he bent over and scooped her up, as well. "I'll take the girls to the kitchen. You take care of Josh. Nico, you want to come?"

The boy didn't need a second invitation. He launched himself out of the tub and hurried over to Nate's side so fast he expected to see cartoon swirls of dust behind him.

Grace and Jennifer each let out another wail as he walked out of the bathroom, but as soon as he got to the kitchen, they simultaneously stopped crying. As if someone had flipped a switch in their little minds. He jiggled them on his lap, which made them laugh. So he kept doing it and they kept laughing.

"Sounds like someone is having fun." Mia came into the kitchen, her arm around Josh, who was leaning against her.

"How is he?" Nate asked, jiggling the girls again.

"I'll have to call and cancel the appointment." She blew out a frustrated sigh and Nate felt her disappointment. "Do you mind watching the girls for a few more minutes while I get Josh settled?" she asked.

"No. We're okay here."

Mia's grateful smile made him feel like quite the white knight. When she left he bounced his legs again. The girls laughed again, each one reaching for the other, their hands tangling together.

He smiled at their antics. Something unique about twins. Twice the fun and twice the work. But still kind of neat. Jennifer reached up to grab at his hair. "Yeah. I know. I need a haircut."

Above him a door closed and he heard Mia come down the stairs leading into the kitchen. He looked up at her, once again feeling a flash of sympathy for the weariness etched on her features. "Is he going to be okay?"

"A stomach bug is no fun, but yes—I just hope we don't all get it." She wrapped her arms around her midsection, looking at Nico, her concern clearly expressed in her frown.

Nico seemed to pick up on that, and immediately ran back upstairs.

Nate watched him go, jiggling the girls again as he struggled with an idea. He put the girls down on the floor, watched to make sure they weren't going to get into trouble and then turned back to Mia. He took her hands in his, then leaned forward and brushed a kiss over her forehead.

"I couldn't resist," he whispered, touching her cheek with his forefinger.

A smile teased Mia's lips and he had to fight the urge to brush a kiss over them again. Instead he focused on what she needed more. Correction, what Nico needed.

Don't do it. Don't offer. You don't know anything about kids.

The voice in his head created a hesitation, then saw the concern clearly etched on Mia's features. What else could he do? She was stuck.

"I don't think you should miss that appointment," Nate said, his hand lingering on her shoulder. "Nico has made few strides and I think you need to talk to the doc about that."

"I do, too, but what can I do about Josh?"

"I'll watch him." The words popped out before he could stop them.

"No. You don't need to do this. It's fine. I'll figure something out."

"What? Evangeline and Denny are both working. And you can't take Josh along."

Mia opened her mouth to form her automatic objection, which Nate stopped by simply placing his finger on her lips.

"It will be fine," he said, fighting down his own concerns. It was just one afternoon. He could handle this. "I have a good book to read—your book club book, by the way."

"Were you thinking of coming?"

"I might. If I get it done," Nate returned with a cheeky grin. "Which will probably only happen if I'm stuck in the house babysitting." He squeezed her hand in assurance. "If he sleeps, how hard can this be?"

Mia pressed her lips together, and though she gave him a grateful smile, he sensed her lingering concern.

"Okay. I accept."

Nate looked down at the twins who, thankfully, seemed more than content to pull themselves up on the kitchen chairs. "And you can throw in one of those, too," he said impulsively, as if he was purchasing groceries.

Mia laughed then shook her head. "I'll take the girls. Taking care of Josh will be more than enough for you." She wobbled a moment as Jennifer, giving up on the kitchen chair, tried to climb up her leg.

"He'll be sleeping, I imagine," Nate said. "And I must disagree with your idea that I can't take care of more than one kid while you can take care of three."

Mia gave him a wry grin. "I grew into the job."

"So. Crash course for me," he said, reaching into his pocket and pulling out a quarter. "So heads I take Grace, tails you take Jennifer."

"What?"

He flipped the coin while she was trying to figure

it out and showed it to her with a triumphant gesture. "Heads. I got Grace."

"But… That isn't how it should work," Mia said, bending over to pick Jennifer up.

"My game. My rules." He glanced over at Grace, who was slapping her hands on the chair, then turned back to Mia. "I want to do this." He put extra emphasis on the word want, hoping she understood the subtext.

She still looked as if she wanted to argue with him. So he did the one thing he figured would make her stop talking.

He bent over and kissed her. Then he stroked the short strands of hair back from her adorable pixie face and cupped her chin with his rough hand. "So. Now that we've got that settled. What should I give Josh when he wakes up?"

Mia's eyes grew warmer. Nate couldn't stop himself. He kissed her again.

"Um… You can give him some…some soup. I think there's a can…" She fluttered her hand in the direction of the kitchen cupboards, looking so adorably flustered Nate couldn't help but smile.

"Soup. Got it. And what about this cherub?" he asked, indicating Grace.

Fifteen minutes and a dozen instructions later, Mia was ready to go. Nico, however, clung to Nate's hand as Mia settled Jennifer into the car seat.

"C'mon, honey, we need to go," Mia said, reaching out to Nico, who shook his head.

Nate, still holding Grace, knelt down beside him. "Hey, buddy, you cowboy up and go with your mom. When you get back you and me will go for a long ride."

Nico heaved a dramatic sigh and trudged over to Mia's side.

"Are you sure?" she asked one more time.

"Yeah. I'm sure." Though he wanted to give her another kiss, he contented himself with squeezing her shoulder. "It will be fine."

She gave him a quick smile and covered his hand with hers. "Thanks so much," she said.

"You better go." He took a step away, wrapping his arms around Grace's chubby body and giving her a quick bounce.

She laughed, but then as Mia started walking away, her lower lip trembled and tears welled up in her eyes.

"It's okay, Gracie," he said, bouncing her the way he had before. "She'll be back. I hope."

But the little girl started crying even harder.

Had he done the right thing?

Could he do this?

Chapter Twelve

Mia pulled onto the road leading back to the ranch, fighting the urge to put the accelerator to the floor. She had called Nate a couple of times on her way home from Cranbrook but he hadn't answered. She knew she had to let go, but leaving him with Josh and Grace had created unease on so many levels.

Things were changing between them. She knew her feelings for him grew stronger each moment they spent together.

But misgivings rose up with each mile she'd driven away from the ranch. What if, by taking care of two of her kids, he realized what he might be getting into? What if he realized that he had made a colossal error?

She shot a quick glance behind her at the other half of her family. Jennifer was playing with her feet and Nico was staring out the window.

He needs stability now more than at any other time, Dr. Schuler had said. Keep doing what you're doing. Obviously, something is working.

Mia made that final turn, trying to put her misgivings where they belonged. She parked the van and as soon as she opened the door, Nico barreled out and ran as fast as he could up the sidewalk toward the house. Mia took Jennifer out of the car seat and followed.

"We're back," she called out, dropping the diaper bag with a *thunk* on the kitchen table. She paused, listening, but the only sound was Nico's feet pounding back down the stairs. He stopped in the kitchen, looking puzzled as he lifted his hands in a gesture of confusion.

"Isn't Josh upstairs?" Mia asked as she set Jennifer on the floor.

Nico shook his head and ran past her to the door.

Had Josh gotten suddenly worse? Had Nate driven him to the hospital in Hartley Creek? Had something happened to Grace?

"Wait, buddy. I don't want you going outside without me," Mia said breathlessly. *Don't panic. It's probably fine.*

Nico stopped at the door leading outside, his hand on the knob, clearly waiting for her.

"I'm coming, I'm coming." She grabbed Jennifer again, parked her on her hip and followed Nico out the door on rubbery legs, wishing she didn't feel so breathless, her vulnerability at what she had already lost screeching to the fore. She suspected Josh was somewhere on the yard, but common sense couldn't seem to calm her panic.

Relax. It's fine, she told herself as she scanned the yard, walking toward the barn.

Then she heard the sound of Josh's giggling and Nate's low voice coming from the barn. She sucked in a grateful breath, feeling suddenly weightless. *Thank You, Lord.*

She pulled in another breath, willing her pounding

heart to slow. Nico was already in the barn and as Mia followed him she saw Josh standing beside Nate, who had Grace on his shoulders.

They were watching Nola and her colt.

Nate looked down just as Nico joined them, grabbing on to Nate's elbow.

"Hey, buddy, you're home early." Then he looked up and Mia felt the second their gazes connected. His smile softened, his eyes grew warm. "Welcome back."

He was smiling. He was happy. The kids were fine.

Mia's worries slipped off her shoulders and as she walked toward him she felt as if her feet hardly touched the ground.

"We were trying to figure out what to call the colt," Nate said as she joined him. He lowered one hand and surreptitiously touched her elbow, creating a little thrill of expectation. She felt like a giddy teenager meeting her boyfriend in school. Wanting to touch, but not daring to do too much in front of their friends.

She turned her attention back to her oldest boy. "Hey, Josh, how are you feeling?" she asked, brushing his hair back from his face. He still looked flushed and pale, but he was grinning as he kept his eyes fixed on the colt.

"Nate said I had to stay in bed, but I was tired of sleeping," he said, shooting her a quick glance. "And I wanted to see the colt again."

"Hope that's okay," Nate said, his tone apologetic. "I thought fresh air might do him good. We, uh, also spent some time on the swing that Denny put up the other day."

Mia nodded, looking up at Grace perched on Nate's shoulders. Her face was streaked with dirt and bits of straw clung to her hair, but she was clapping her hands, laughing at the antics of the colt.

"Thanks again," she said, a remarkable feeling of well-being washing over her. He didn't seem flustered at all and the kids were happy.

"I had a good time," he said, giving her a quick wink. "I'd do it again."

"That's great because Evangeline, Renee and I were talking about a girls-only cruise down the Panama..."

"Well, you girls just keep talking," he said. "Cause Renee and Evangeline will have to convince Zach and Denny to babysit, too. They might not be as willing. Just saying." He gave her a wink, which made her laugh, which made Jennifer, sitting on her hip laugh, as well.

"Have you decided on a name yet?" she asked.

"I want to call it Flash or Lightning. Because I think he will be a fast horse," Josh said.

They watched awhile and then Jennifer started fussing and rubbing at her eyes with her pudgy hands. "I better bring this little one in the house," Mia said, giving her a quick hug. "She's exhausted."

"I think Grace can use a nap, too," Nate added. "She hasn't slept since you left. We had a real busy afternoon, didn't we?" He grinned at Grace and rubbed her nose with his.

Mia's heart melted at the sight. Then he glanced her way and his eyebrows lifted as if curious what she was thinking.

She simply smiled, brushing her lips over Jennifer's soft hair.

"C'mon, boys, we have to lay the girls down."

"I don't want to." Josh's voice wavered up and down in a classic whine.

Mia was about to reprimand him when Nate, still holding Grace, crouched down in front of him.

"Hey, buddy, you're still sick," Nate said, dropping one hand on the boy's shoulder. "And Nico gets to come back outside because he had to go with your mom to Cranbrook while you got to stay here and play outside with me and Grace. You go have a nap and when you're done, you can come back outside again."

Josh was about to protest when he caught Nate's warning frown. He slumped his shoulders, pushed his hands in his pockets and slouched outside, Nico trailing alongside him.

Mia watched them go, surprised at the mixture of emotions she felt watching the exchange. The mother part of her wanted to intervene, yet as she watched Nate deal with Josh, she felt a combination of relief and release. For the first time in years she felt like someone had her back.

Nate caught her look and lifted a hand in apology. "Sorry. I shouldn't have taken over. He's your kid."

"No. It's okay. You spent the morning with him. You had every right to have expectations from him," Mia assured.

"I guess it's just the trainer in me," he said as they followed the boys across the yard. "Can't seem to keep my nose out."

"Well, I'll try not to kick or bite you when you get too close," Mia said with a laugh as he opened the door of the house for her.

"Just bare your teeth in warning if you're going to, or flatten your ears and I'll step out of your way."

Mia laughed again, feeling more lighthearted in the past few moments than she had in months.

Then Grace fussed and Mia reached out for her.

"It's okay. I got her," Nate said, shifting the little girl on his hip.

As he did, Mia pointed to his shoulder. "You ripped your coat."

Nate moved his shoulder to see better, then grimaced. "Oh, no. And that's my lucky coat."

"Lucky?"

"Well, it's the one I've worn to all the competitions I've won. I guess I'll have to fix it."

"And how handy are you with a needle and thread?" she asked.

"Needle and thread?" Nate scoffed. "Real men use duct tape."

Mia laughed. "Bring it over to the house when you don't need it and I'll fix it for you," she said.

Nate gave her an odd look. "Really?"

"Yeah. Evangeline has a sewing machine. I can fix it with that."

"You really are a woman of many talents," he said, dropping an arm over her shoulders. He cupped her face and smiled down at her. "You'll make some guy very happy someday."

It was a casual gesture, but behind it lay the kisses they had shared. The moments they had stolen.

Then he caught her hand, his expression growing serious. "We need to talk," he said.

"Sounds serious." She forced herself to smile, but dread clutched at her as she held his eyes.

"It is."

"So talk."

His eyes slipped to the boys running ahead of them,

the girls they carried. "Not now," he said. "Not in front of the kids."

"Of course." She managed another smile, but as they walked to the house, she couldn't stop a niggle of unease at the tone in his voice, at the use of the words *some guy*. Not him? And when he didn't kiss her again, that niggle slowly twisted at her heart.

"Good as new," Mia said to herself as she snipped the last of the threads on Nate's coat. Or at least as new as it was before it got ripped. He had dropped it off yesterday and only today had she a chance to fix it.

The sleeves had a permanent kink in the elbow. The hem was ragged. But it smelled of Nate and outside. She held the coat close a moment, as if holding its owner. It had been years since she'd done something so domestic as mending clothing for a man. Al was always ripping something and she was always fixing it for him.

Anger rose up at thoughts of Al. The old feelings of betrayal and loss. She looked down at Nate's jacket, her anger morphing into the same uncertainty that always accompanied thoughts of Nate.

Her children's own biological father didn't want them, why would Nate?

She looked over the coat once more then noticed a hole in the one pocket. May as well fix that, too. She slipped the coat back under the pressure foot and started sewing, a feeling of housewifely satisfaction washing over her.

The twins were playing on the floor and Nico and Josh were outside helping Nate build the birdhouses. The feeling that someone else was taking care of her responsibility was new to her. At the same time, she felt as if things were gathering together, bringing her to a place in her life she had never dared allow herself to go.

Mia reversed the stitching to tie it off, then pulled the coat out from the machine. As she did, a piece of paper slid out of the pocket and onto the floor.

She bent over to pick it up and saw Lacy's name in sparkly pink pen followed by her phone number and the words, "Call me. I'm available Wednesday to Friday."

The unease she had felt previously returned. Though she wanted to think it might simply be a flirty young girl coming on to a good-looking guy, her mind flicked back to Sunday, a week and a half ago. Nate talking to Lacy. Taking something from her.

She got up and set the jacket aside. She was going to wait until suppertime tonight to give him his jacket, but a sudden urgency gripped her. She needed to see him. Now.

She ran upstairs, changed into a skirt, flicked some mascara on her eyelashes, some lipstick on her mouth and spritzed some perfume on her neck. Then she went and got the girls ready. Ten minutes later she had the girls in the stroller, Nate's jacket hanging over it. As she walked she forced herself to think about Nate. Think about the kisses they shared.

Think about what he had said. She had to believe that he truly cared about her. That he was willing to take on her children. If she didn't, then everything would be for nothing.

"So how much do you charge for babysitting?" Denny asked Nate as he handed Josh another nail. "I've got to go pick up Ella in a few minutes, maybe you can watch her while I go check the cows."

The pounding of hammers reverberated through the cool of the garage as Nico and Josh flailed away, brows furrowed, lips pressed as they concentrated on putting the birdhouses together.

"Heard you did a great job the other morning with the kids," Denny continued, obviously not done with his little joke.

"Be careful you don't bang your thumb," Nate said to Nico as he held the rough boards at right angles for Nico, choosing to ignore Denny's lame humor. "We want to make sure these birdhouses are good and strong."

"We're good for the money," Denny added, giving Nate an elbow. "You're always saying how broke you are."

"What is broke?" Josh asked, sitting back on his heels and wiping a bead of sweat off his forehead. He still looked flushed, but happy to be spending time with Nate and Denny and Nico after his sleep this morning.

"Broke is what Nate doesn't have to be," Denny said, his oblique comment making Nate sigh. He knew Denny was referring to the estate from his late step-father.

"It's not that easy, Denny, and you know it," Nate retorted.

"It's also not that hard. Don't you get tired of letting your past determine your future?"

Nate stifled a sigh. "If I take that money, then the past will determine my future. I need to make it on my own."

"It's only money. The guy is gone. Dead. Expired."

"What does expired mean?" Josh asked.

"What this conversation is," Nate said, shooting

Denny a warning glance. "So, looks like you've got the front nailed to the sides already," Nate said, lifting up the frame Josh had nailed together. "Now you just have to put the back on."

"One of the guys driving a truck for me was on the two-way this afternoon, yapping about a place up Coal Creek way. Eighty acres with a small house and training barn and corrals."

"I heard."

Denny frowned. "How?"

"You're not the only one with connections," he said, handing Josh the back of the birdhouse. "Lacy Miedema told me. A week ago on Sunday. Guess it belongs to her dad and he's thinking of selling."

Denny nudged him in the side. "Interested?"

Nate brushed him off with a shrug. "It might be a place to rent."

"Why bother renting? Why don't you buy it?"

The idea wasn't new to Nate. Ever since he kissed Mia, he'd been teetering between two emotions.

Fear and peace.

If he bought that place, it meant making a commitment to staying, which meant opening himself completely and wholly to Mia. Letting her take over the space in his heart he had guarded all these years.

At the same time the idea generated an unexpected peace. The thought of a place of his own. A family of his own.

"You don't need to look so worried about this." It was more Denny's tone than his comment that bespoke a knowledge of the inner workings of Nate's mind. "You don't have to run out and make this decision today."

"I know." Nate couldn't stop the testy tone from

creeping into his voice. Then he gave Denny an apologetic look. "Sorry. I didn't mean to snap. I just feel like things are coming at me so fast."

"Life happens that way sometimes," Denny agreed. "Sometimes God shifts you in unexpected directions, but when you arrive, you realize this is where you should be. I wouldn't trade with anyone and I don't regret anything that happened to me along the way."

The conviction in his voice eased Nate's own trepidation.

"I get it," Nate said. "I was supposed to be at Arden Charles's ranch right now. Working with him and learning from him. Fine-tuning Tango for the competition. Instead, I'm here."

"But you can leave soon, now, can't you? Tango is well enough and you can divide up your horse trailer and keep the colt and Nola separate from the rest?"

Denny's tone was casual, but Nate understood the deeper question. *Are you still going?*

Nate chewed at his lower lip, then pushed himself to his feet, walking a ways away from the boys. Denny followed as Nate leaned against the workbench behind him.

"Tell me what's on your mind," Denny said.

Nate's glance ticked from Denny to the boys then he eased out a sigh. "For the past five years, I've had a plan—a solid plan—and getting Tango to the futurity, having Nola and Bella foal, was all part of that. Then I came here. Then I met Mia…." He let the sentence trail off, not sure how to convey the confusion of feelings that circulated through his mind each time he thought of her.

"You care about her, don't you?"

Nate shoved his hand through his hair, blowing out a sigh. "Scares the living daylights out of me, but I do."

"What scares you?"

Nate waited a moment, self-preservation and years of being on his own slowing his response.

"I'm scared of opening my heart. To her and to the kids," he said, his voice lowered so the boys couldn't hear. "I'm scared of what could happen to me if she pushes me away. If she doesn't want me."

"I've seen how she looks at you. Evangeline has said that Mia is a different person since she's met you. In spite of what happened to her, she seems happier. More settled."

Denny's words kindled a hope in his soul that he had kept banked for so many years. The hope of a person to share his life with and the hope of a family.

"That's what I'm struggling with. I know how important it is to support the people who depend on me. That's why this competition is so important to me. If I can get a stake together, I might have a chance…" He let the sentence trail off, still afraid of vocalizing the half-formed thoughts that plagued him each night before he fell asleep. Thoughts about Mia and a future.

"I feel like I need space to catch my breath. Figure out what I want. My focus has been this futurity for so long—I need to compete."

Silence followed that comment and Nate knew how it sounded, but he also knew the fear that had made him say it.

"So you're still leaving?" Denny asked.

"I have to."

"Well, you gotta do what you gotta do, I guess."

"I gotta do what's best for me."

"Of course you do."

Nate heard the disappointment in Denny's voice and struggled to separate himself from it. He had always respected his brother. But he had been on his own for the past few years. He had never had to think of anyone else or work anyone into his life.

He crouched down to pet his dog, giving himself a moment to respond to Denny's last remark.

Socks looked at him, but then Josh called him and he trotted over.

"Would you come back?" Denny asked quietly, as if speaking too loudly might scare Nate off.

Nate held that idea, letting it sink into his soul and then he smiled. "That is my new plan."

Denny's shoulders lowered as if he had been holding his own tension in. "That's good to know. So, next question. Would your winnings be enough for you to buy that place you looked at?"

"No."

"I know you don't want to hear it, but there's a solution to this."

Nate shot him an angry look but Denny seemed undeterred.

"I think you need to put Karl where he belongs," Denny said, his voice quiet, as if he understood how difficult this was for Nate. "I think you need to put him in the past. In the ground where he is right now. This money is a gift. As long as you think taking money from Karl gives him power over you, he still wins. Even from the grave."

The only sound in the quiet that followed was the uneven ringing of the boys' hammers on the nails. Nate swallowed back the immediate defense of his position, reality nipping at his heels like a pesky cow-dog.

"I think there was a reason you ended up here," Denny continued. "Let God use that. Let yourself accept what is happening to you. I know how scary it can be. I had the same thing with Evangeline and Ella. I had to go through my own journey and I suspect you're partway through yours. Mia is a wonderful, loving person. She, of all people, would not give her heart and loyalty lightly." Denny nudged him with an elbow. "Or her kisses."

The light note eased some of the heaviness away and Nate laughed. "We've had a few of those."

"And I know Mia. She is not the type of person to let someone easily into her life. If she has let you get close it's because she trusts you. Which means you can trust her. And it also means you have to be careful with her."

"I know that, too," Nate replied. "So I want you to make sure you keep everything we've said right now to yourself."

"Of course." Then Denny clapped him on the shoulder, a brisk way of saying that for now, he was leaving this discussion alone. "Let's go help the boys finish up those birdhouses. Evangeline said we needed to eat early because they've got book club tonight. You going?"

"No. I want to work with Tango after supper."

"Perfect. That gives me an excuse to get out of the house, too. Book club always gives me the heebie-jeebies." Denny shuddered. "You think about what I said. You pray about it. And know that I'd love to have my brother close by."

Nate toyed with that thought as a glimpse of a future

he never thought available to him hovered at the edges
of his thoughts. Family. Community.

Mia.

Then Josh and Nico looked up at him as they walked
over. Both smiled.

And Nate felt the warmth of their affection. And he
allowed that glimpse of a future with them and Mia to
become more real.

Chapter Thirteen

"So you're still leaving?"

Mia was about to enter the garage when she heard Denny asking Nate the same question she never dared ask.

"I have to," Nate was saying.

Mia paused, her feet suddenly frozen in place. She couldn't move ahead.

"Well, you gotta do what you gotta do, I guess," was Denny's quiet reply.

"I gotta do what's best for me," Nate said with a sense of finality.

Why were her hands tingling like this? Why couldn't she move her feet?

But she had to. Had to get out of here. Had to leave.

Thankfully, the girls were quiet as she dragged the stroller backward out of the rut, got it turned around and headed toward the house. Crazy girl, she thought, her feet beating a rhythm in time to the words pounding through her head. *Crazy, romantic, foolish girl. Why did you think he would want to stay with you when he had a chance with someone like Lacy?*

She needed to keep her feet moving to prevent her mind from taking over. So instead of going to the house, she continued down the driveway toward the road, her pace picking up. Evangeline would be coming home soon; she needed to see her friend.

But as she walked other things Nate said wound their insidious way into her head.

"You'll make some guy very happy someday... We need to talk..."

She closed her eyes and shook her head as if to dislodge the words, but they clung and slowly wormed their way into her mind. When Nate said that she foolishly assumed he was talking about them.

Now she realized he was probably finding a way to ease her out of his life.

Had Lacy made him change his mind?

She faltered, tears threatening. She'd been here before—on her own, left behind. She had managed then, she would manage now.

But the thought of Nate leaving created an unyielding ache in her heart.

Dear Lord, please help me get through this, was all she could pray. *Carry me and my kids because I keep coming back to the truth that only You are faithful.*

She walked for another fifteen minutes, thankful that the girls had fallen asleep, but still having seen no sign of Evangeline. So she turned around and returned to the house. The boys were still busy in the garage when she came back. She brought the girls, one at a time, into the house and when she came back from laying them down she noticed a blinking light on the phone. Evangeline had left a message saying that she wouldn't be home until it was time for book club. She would pick up some treats from the bakery. Could Mia feed Nate and Denny the burritos she had planned?

Mia dropped the phone onto the cradle and dragged her hands over her face. She didn't want to see Nate right now. But she had no choice. So with heavy feet she started frying hamburger and cutting up peppers and onions.

While she was assembling the burritos she heard the pounding of feet, the door slamming open, Josh complaining.

What was going on?

Denny burst into the house carrying both Josh and Nico. "Sorry. Gotta run," he said, panting as he deposited the boys on the kitchen floor. "The cows are out." And without another word he turned around and left. Mia hurried to the porch, Josh and Nico on her heels.

Cows milled about the yard, bawling; calves scurried around, kicking up dust, then racing off as if enjoying their newfound freedom. She saw Denny skirting the herd, heading toward the corral, legs pumping.

Through the dust of the cows' hooves on the packed yard, she saw Nate in the corral saddling Tango with quick, brisk movements. He was all business. He looked up and for a moment she thought he was looking at her. She couldn't help her reaction. She pulled back.

"C'mon, boys. We better get inside," she said, tugging on their arms.

"But we want to watch," Josh whined.

"It's too dangerous," she insisted.

Then she heard a sound from Nico. Her gaze shot to her son who was leaning forward, his hands stretched out to Nate. The noise he made had an urgency. As if he was afraid for Nate.

And in spite of the joy she felt at Nico's hesitant step to communication, a sense of foreboding loomed.

He would be okay, she told herself. Nate knew how to take care of himself.

It was her own heart she had to guard. Her own life she had to watch over, she thought as she pulled the boys back into the house. Then, in spite of the drama unfolding outside, she managed to get them fed and the girls bathed and got the boys watching a movie.

Half an hour later she heard Evangeline drive up and Mia ran out to meet her. Thankfully, the bawling noise had settled down and Mia saw Denny and Nate herding the cows back through the gate to the pasture.

Evangeline was taking boxes out of the back of the car. Mia assumed these were treats for the book club meeting.

"Let me take that," Mia said to Evangeline. "You take care of Ella."

"That'd be great," Evangeline said, tilting the box toward her. "Anyone from book club here yet?"

"Not yet. Let's get into the house before the cows get any closer."

Evangeline glanced over her shoulder as she carried Ella to the house. "How did they get out?"

"I don't know. Denny and Nate have been busy the past half hour getting them back in."

Evangeline pulled Ella out of the car seat and followed Mia into the house.

"And how was your day?" Evangeline asked as she shifted Ella and grabbed a glass of water. "You get to spend any more time with Nate?"

The painful throb made a return visit. Mia forced herself to smile and shake her head. She wanted more than anything to sit and talk things through with Evangeline, but now was not the time. Especially not when the door of the porch creaked open and Sophie Brouwer and Eloise Beck strolled into the kitchen.

"Sorry we're early, but we wanted so badly to see your place," Sophie was saying as she set her book bag on the table. She looked around and then her gaze landed on Mia. "Oh, my dear girl. How are you coping? Have you settled anything with the insurance company yet?"

Mia felt another tremble of emotion and simply gave Mrs. Beck a quick smile. "I'll find out tomorrow," was all she allowed herself to say. "And I'm sorry, but I need to excuse myself to get the boys in bed."

"Of course, honey, we can talk later." And as Mia shut off the television and took her reluctant sons up the stairs she heard Eloise saying to Evangeline, "Did Lacy talk to you about coming tonight?"

Mia's step faltered and she clung to the banister as Evangeline said yes. *Oh, dear Lord, I can't face her. Not now,* Mia prayed, feeling small and petty and nervous all at the same time.

"Are you coming, Mommy?" Josh asked, pulling on her arm. She gave him a quick hug, as if to anchor herself to her present. Her children needed her. She had to forget about what she needed.

And as she tucked the boys in later and prayed with them, she clung to the faith that had sustained her through other dark times in her life.

Help me to trust in Your unfailing love, she prayed as Josh recited his usual bedtime prayer. *Help me to be thankful for what I have. For my children. Help me to take care of them. To put You first in my life, and then them.*

But even as she prayed, a voice echoed a wish for someone to take care of her.

She took a slow breath, started down the stairs and came to a full stop halfway down.

From here she saw Lacy Miedema standing in the kitchen, chatting with Evangeline as she helped her put the treats on a plate.

Today, Lacy wore a blue tank top covered with a filmy white blouse with large, pale blue polka dots, tucked into slim-fitting blue jeans. Ropes of various silver necklaces hung down her neck, bangle earrings flashed from her ears. On her narrow feet she wore gladiator sandals. She looked fashionably adorable with her loosely curled blond hair flowing over her shoulders. Young and cute and fresh.

In spite of her own skirt and makeup, Mia felt old and dowdy and tired just looking at her.

She took a breath and was about to go down the stairs when the porch door opened and Nate stepped inside the kitchen. A bright smile lit up Lacy's face.

"Hello, Nate. Nice to see you again." Lacy tilted her head to one side, her hair flowing across her shoulder in an artlessly flirtatious gesture. "How is Nola's foal?"

Lacy knew about Nola's baby. Mia had treasured that moment as something special between her and Nate.

Mia clutched the banister as the implications of that sank in. He and Lacy had talked before. And why not? He had her number in the pocket of his jacket with a note that said "call me."

Mia shoved her rough hands with their ragged fingernails behind her back and slouched down the stairs, trying not to draw attention to herself. Nate had his back to her as he sampled some of the goodies that Lacy had arranged on the plate. Mia slipped around the corner and dropped into the nearest chair. Jeff sat beside her, but he and Angie were laughing at something he was showing her in the book they were to discuss.

Mia didn't want to listen to Nate and Lacy, but it was as if every nerve in her body was tingling with awareness.

"I don't know if I'll have time. I've got a futurity to get ready for," Nate was saying to her.

Mia's heart skipped as she tried to still the sudden panic his words had created, reminding her of what he had said this morning.

"I'm thinking of attending," Lacy was saying.

"It's a great competition, if you're interested in cutting horses."

"Interested? I'm addicted. I have some horses at my father's place. Doc Bar and San Peppy are in their pedigree."

"Wow. Cutting Horse who's who." Nate sounded full of admiration. Lacy obviously spoke Nate's language. Was obviously not as afraid of horses as Mia was.

A perfect match for him.

"I'd love to see your horse Tango, if I may?" Lacy was asking. "He might be a good stud for my mares."

"Sure. I need to talk to you, anyway," Nate was saying.

Mia sat on her hands, pressing her lips together, fighting down her self-doubt. Then the sound of the outside door falling cut off Nate and Lacy's voices. They were gone.

"So, Mia, what did you think of the book?" Jeff was asking her.

She blinked, pulling her attention back from Nate and Lacy to Jeff, who was watching her, his brown eyes crinkling around the edges with suppressed humor.

"I liked it," she said.

"In spite of the happy ending? I know you think those are hokey."

Mia shrugged away his question, not sure what to think of happy endings right now when she felt as if she was in the middle of her own unhappy one.

She looked out the living room window. From here she saw part of the yard. She caught a flash of white and saw Lacy going into the barn. Nate right behind her.

All her insecurities and self-doubts plodded through her mind with leaden feet and the longer Lacy stayed away from the meeting, the heavier her conviction grew that she needed to do something about this. Needed to take charge of her life.

Maybe she and her family needed some time away from all of this.

"Forget the former things. Do not dwell on the past. See I am making a new thing." Nate ran his finger along the words of Isaiah as if to absorb them, once again, into his being.

Since he had come here his life had taken many quick twists and turns, dragging him to a new place.

Nate sat back in his chair, feeling like he had to catch his breath. It had been a long, busy day. This morning he had met Lacy Miedema at her father's place and had walked over the yard. It wasn't the perfect spot, but it had a lot of potential. Then he had gone to the bank to see about financing.

Finally, he talked to the lawyer in Calgary.

Yesterday, he had been so uncertain as to what he should do. But after talking to Denny, hearing his reassuring words made him realize that he was letting his past dictate his present. He could stay on the sidelines of life, guarding his heart, or he could take a chance.

A chance with Mia. He had wanted to talk to her, to carefully feel her out about how things stood between them, but he hadn't seen her all day. She had been busy, as well. Maybe after supper, once the kids were in bed, they'd have a chance to talk.

Maybe steal a few more kisses.

The thought put a smile on his lips.

"Nate, you in here?" Denny's voice echoing in the hallway of the trailer made him jump. He stopped in the entrance to the living room, his hands on his hips. "Evangeline wants to know if you're coming for supper."

"Be right there," Nate said, pushing off his chair. "Just let me wash up."

"So did you go to the Miedema place?" Denny asked as he followed him to the washroom. "What did you think?"

"It's nice. Almost perfect," Nate said as he soaped up his hands. "The house is a bit small and the arena needs work, but it's a great location."

"Price?"

Nate grabbed a towel, thinking once again about the financial aspect of his life. "If I use Karl's money I could swing it."

Denny leaned one shoulder against the doorframe,

folding his arms over his chest as if settling in for a man-to-man chat. "So you're taking the money?"

Nate held that question a moment, hefting the weight of it. Trying to separate the man from the money. "I think I might. Unless things go really bad here."

"How bad could they go? I think Mia's pretty crazy about you and her kids like you just as much." Denny was quiet a moment. "And Nico is already coming around. Maybe he just needs to know there's some stability in his life."

Nate smiled at that as he hung up the towel. "I think so, too. And I hope for Mia's sake as much as Nico's that we're right."

"You know, you'll do fine with this whole thing," he said. "Besides, me and Evangeline are here. Mia's got lots of good friends. There's a lot of support available for you."

"That makes all the difference."

"So you think you're going to call the real-estate agent tomorrow?"

"I'll probably head into town. See if I can do a deal. I need to go to Calgary, too, to sign everything to do with Karl's estate."

"That's great." Denny gave him a lopsided smile as if he couldn't believe that Nate was actually taking his advice.

"Really. Like you said, Karl has had too much influence in my life," Nate said. "I want to make other plans."

"So glad to hear that." Denny clapped his hand on his shoulder. "I could use your help the next couple months. Evangeline is pulling out all the stops on this wedding. My sisters won't hold her back and I'll need the moral support of a brother."

Nate laughed as he pulled open the door of the trailer. "I think I could do that for you," he said as they walked across the yard.

They stepped into the house to be greeted by the smell of supper cooking. Denny walked over to Evangeline standing by the stove, stirring something in a pot and gave her a kiss. Nate looked around, listening.

The only sound he heard was Ella burbling in the living room, playing with her toys.

"Where's Mia?" he asked, looking over a table set for only four people.

Evangeline glanced over her shoulder. "She said she had to go to town and that she would be treating the kids to supper there."

That was puzzling. But so was the fact that she had dropped his coat off at the trailer without stopping to talk to him yesterday. He had hoped to talk to Mia last night, but it didn't work out so he had hoped to do so tonight. He wanted to talk to her about his tentative plans. Feel her out about their future.

And as the night progressed, Mia still stayed away, making Evangeline fretful and Nate puzzled.

When the phone finally rang at about nine-thirty, he jumped. Evangeline answered it.

When she came back she was frowning. "That was Mia," she said. "She's staying at Renee and Zach's place tonight. She said something about needing to see the insurance people tomorrow. I guess she heard today that the money is finally being paid out. Renee had said she would babysit for her."

"Is she back tomorrow?" Nate asked, wondering why she hadn't thought he could babysit for her.

"No. She said she hadn't seen her parents in a few months and her sister and brother-in-law are up for a visit, so she hoped to connect with them, as well. She said she might not be back until Saturday."

"Saturday?" Nate asked. "Why so long?"

"Nelson's about three hours from here. I can't see that she would come back right away." Evangeline sat down on the edge of the chair she had been lounging in just a few moments ago. "Did you know she was going?" she asked Nate.

He shook his head, wondering why Mia hadn't told him. Technically, he didn't have any right to know her comings and goings, but still. He thought they had an understanding.

Mia didn't call again that night, nor did she call him or Evangeline the next day. He tried to send her a couple of text messages, but she didn't respond to either.

Nate dragged himself through the next few days. He spent some time with Tango, doing dry work without the cows. He was pleased with Tango's progress. He stopped deep and drew back well. His sweeps were clean without any hesitation. He was as ready as he could be.

And each time his cell phone chimed, he jumped. One was a call from Lacy, asking him if he could come to her father's place to look at her horses, but he put her off. One was a call from Arden that Nate let go to voice mail. Arden had said that he was looking forward to him coming and working with him and his horses. As he contemplated what he had once planned, plans that had been subdued to whispers the past few days grew to shouts the longer Mia stayed away.

He also got a phone call from Karl's lawyer's office confirming his appointment. No matter what happened with Mia, Denny was right. He may as well take Karl's money and make it his own.

By the time Saturday came his frustration and disappointment had melded into anger. Maybe he didn't deserve an explanation, but he thought he had made fairly clear that she mattered to him.

Obviously, the same wasn't true for her.

He felt his old anger return.

The past few weeks, life had sent him down roads he hadn't chosen. He thought he had come to a good place. And now?

Now it seemed time to take control of his life again. Be the one in charge. He needed to take Tango out on a ride. He strode around the barn, heading for the corral just as a minivan pulled onto the yard. He came to a halt as Mia got out, but she didn't see him.

The boys, however, did and as the other side door opened, Nico exploded out of the van, running toward him, arms outstretched.

Nate felt like a knife had been plunged into his stomach. Unsure of what to do, Nate stayed where he was, not moving. Nico's steps faltered and he came to a halt when he saw that Nate wasn't coming toward him. Socks, however, was under no such restraint and ran straight to the boy, prancing around him, tongue hanging out with eager expectation. Nate saw the question in the boy's eyes as Nico absently petted Socks and it turned the knife.

Did he dare reconnect with the boys until he knew what was going on with Mia?

"Nico. Josh. Come back here," he heard Mia calling out as she lifted Jennifer out of the van.

She looked over at him, then away with no word of greeting. No sign that he was even there.

His question was answered.

So he whistled for his dog that looked from him to the boys as if torn, as well. Then Socks obediently trotted toward Nate and followed him back to the barn.

Mia knew Nate was watching her as she carried Jennifer and Grace up to the house. She felt his look, as real as a touch. But she couldn't go to him.

Too easily she remembered how Al's betrayal had cut her.

Nate was no different.

Déjà vu all over again, she realized. And this time it was worse. Al had never mattered to her as much as Nate had. That's why she had left. She needed time away from the situation to find her independence again.

"Can we go see Nate?" Josh asked as he trotted alongside her up the sidewalk. "I want to show him the bow and arrow that Grandpa got me."

"Not right now, honey," Mia said, trying to keep her voice even. Calm. Motherly. Trying not to let the tension at seeing Nate creep into her voice. "I have to get the girls in bed and you and Nico need to get some lunch, then a nap. This afternoon we have to go back into town."

When Mia had called Evangeline this morning to make plans, her friend had said that Nate might be gone this afternoon. Something about him going to Calgary.

So Mia had planned her trip to arrive at noon while he was gone.

But when she saw him standing by the corral her heart dropped into her stomach. She wasn't ready to see him yet.

Then as soon as she brought the girls into the house, they started crying. Josh started whining and Nico sat on the floor, kicking his feet at a chair.

It was as if they had immediately picked up on her mood.

She stepped up the pace, filling sippy cups for the girls, slapping together a quick sandwich for the boys.

"I don't like ham," Josh said, pouting at the bread Mia had put in front of him. Nico's only response was to push the plate away.

Mia bit down her frustration. The past few weeks she had gotten used to having help with her kids. Her parents had been great and before that, Nate…

She cut that thought off. Nate was out there, she was in here. She couldn't face him yet. She had four kids, a fact hammered home every day she spent with her parents and her sister, who couldn't envision having a kid, let alone four kids. The subtext in all of her sister's comments was that four kids was such a huge burden, she couldn't imagine how anyone would choose to take that on. And poor Nico. What an extra trouble. And twins? My, oh my.

All this was said with a smile and a modicum of admiration at how Mia managed, but nonetheless, each sympathetic word struck like an arrow at Mia's own insecurities.

Why would someone like Nate want to take on all this?

The time away from the situation made her see everything more clearly and with less of a romantic eye. Seeing Nate with Lacy was a wake-up call. Mia knew she could never give Nate, or any man, what someone like Lacy could.

She was on her own.

She packed the girls up the stairs, stopping at the top to catch her breath as Grace almost slipped out of her arms. When did they get so heavy? So awkward to carry?

Grace immediately started crying when she got to the bedroom and Jennifer squirmed away from her as she tried to change her.

Just get through this, she reminded herself, biting down on a sudden burst of frustration. *Just do what comes next.*

Finally, she had them ready for their nap and as she closed the door on them, she paused a moment, letting the sudden quiet wash over her. Just a minute, she told herself. Just a few seconds of peace.

Then she heard a thump and a cry from Josh. "No, Nico. You have to stay here."

Stifling a sigh, she pushed herself away to deal with the next crisis.

Nico stood by the porch door as if ready to leave.

"Where are you going?" she asked, walking over to his side and kneeling down beside him.

Nico grunted, pulling on the door. Mia suspected he wanted to go out to see Nate.

"No, honey. You need to finish your lunch and then have a nap. You and Josh." Last night they had stayed up late playing games with Grandpa and Grandma and this morning they'd had an early start. The boys were tired and cranky. "We are going out again this afternoon."

Before she left, she had gotten the good news that the insurance company was going to settle. They needed her to come in today and sign yet another raft of documents and then they could release the money.

And once that was released, she could get on with her life.

Nico protested again, but Mia held her ground.

She convinced them to finish their lunch and lie down on the couch in the living room. She sat with them a moment, fighting her own weariness, wanting nothing more than to join them in a nap.

But she had to get her suitcases from the van and do the laundry she didn't dare do at her parents' apartment.

Finally, their eyes drifted shut, their breathing grew heavy and deep and she dared leave. As she opened the back door her eyes flicked over the yard and she felt a twitch of trepidation when she saw Nate's truck still parked by the trailer. He wasn't gone.

Yet.

She shook her reactions off. She had to stay focused. Once she got the money from the insurance company she could start rebuilding her flower shop and her life.

It was an answer to prayer, that's for sure, she realized.

Next Monday, she had another trip to Cranbrook to see Dr. Schuler to report on the little bit of progress Nico was making.

If you want to call grunts progress.

She opened the van door and bent over to dig out the suitcases. As she set them on the gravel beside the van and reached out to close the door she saw Nate coming toward her. Shock, pain, anger, excitement all charged at her like errant horses, each demanding attention.

She shook the feelings off, reaching back for older feelings. The same ones she felt when Al had left.

You're on your own.

Nate walked around the van and she knew the only way she was going to get through this was to go on the defensive. To be the one in control for a change.

"I imagine you're getting ready to go to the futurity with Tango?" she asked.

Very well done, she heard Other Mother encourage her. *Very confident. Very in charge.*

He looked momentarily taken aback at her offensive move. Then he nodded. "Yeah. I'm leaving."

Mia's hands grew sweaty, clutching the suitcase holding the few clothes her children owned. She had to keep going. "I think that's a good idea. It's what you should do. Leave," she said.

Nate scowled and tilted his head to one side, as if trying to catch her comment from another angle. "What are you saying?"

Mia couldn't hold his steady gaze. Couldn't look into those hazel eyes that seemed to have chilled. Eyes that had, at one time, looked at her with warmth and caring.

Really? Had he? Or was it just her lonely heart that had imagined that?

Did you imagine his kisses?

She pushed those thoughts aside. She had to stay focused.

"I'm saying that it's right that you leave the ranch. That you go."

She saw the questions behind Nate's eyes but she didn't look away. Then he gave a curt nod, as if agreeing, and took a step away from her. "You're saying I should leave?"

Mia felt puzzled herself at his confusion, but then reminded herself that he was the one who said it first.

"It's what you should do," she said. He was a roaming, wandering man and he wouldn't be happy being tied down to her and four children.

His eyes narrowed, but thankfully he said nothing more. He simply turned and strode across the yard, each step he took away from her like a hammer blow.

This is for the best, she reminded herself. She wasn't going to be the one left behind again.

Then why did she feel exactly like that, she wondered as she saw Nate walk to his truck and get inside?

She thought he was going to drive away; instead, she saw him backing up to the horse trailer he'd been working on the past few days. Then he got out and began cranking on the supports, lowering its weight onto the back of his truck.

She drew in a long, slow breath. It was done.

Nate was leaving.

Chapter Fourteen

"C'mon, Tango, it's time to go."

Nate slipped the halter over his horse's head, fighting down the anger blended with anguish that threatened to choke him.

Time to go. Mia had made that fairly clear to him. He should have known, when she took off so unexpectedly, that things were going south. She had underlined that a few moments ago with her encouragement for him to leave.

He wasn't sure what happened to make her want him to leave, but he was sure he didn't want to find out. He didn't need to have her remind him yet again that he wasn't the right guy for her or her kids.

Denny wasn't home to say goodbye to, nor was Evangeline. He knew where Denny was doing his gravel haul; he could probably meet him somewhere. Get him to pass on his farewells and thanks to Evangeline. He felt like a heel, leaving like this, but he knew he would feel worse sticking around, knowing that sooner or later Josh or Nico would come out of the house. Knowing he might see Mia again.

He stopped a moment, steadying himself on the railing as his heart wrenched at the thought of leaving her. Of leaving her kids.

He took a deep breath, sent up a quick prayer for strength. He was on his own again.

This time, though, he felt as if he had help along the way. Denny's thoughts and prayers. A new, rebuilt relationship with God. He would receive the strength he needed to get through this new phase of his life.

It was that thought that kept him moving. Kept him packing up his tack, his clothes, the few things he'd had scattered around the trailer.

Half an hour later the trailer and his truck were packed up. Time to move the horses.

As he walked into the corral, his mind slipped back to the times he had spent with the boys. Those precious moments with Mia watching.

What would his leaving do to them? What would it do to Nico?

He couldn't think that. He had set his face on this path. He had Karl's money coming to him. He had the wherewithal to make a few decisions on his own.

He caught Duke and Bella and tied them up one at a time to the corral fence beside Tango. Then he went into the barn to get Nola. He hoped her colt would follow her out of the barn and into the horse trailer. He wasn't entirely sure how it would go. In a pinch he could first load the colt and then take Nola inside.

He was just coming out of the barn with Nola, her colt tottering behind, when he saw Mia leaving the house with the kids. Yesterday he had toyed with the idea of keeping only enough of Karl's money to put a down payment on the acreage Lacy had shown him and give Mia the rest to start up her flower shop.

But now that her insurance money had gone through, she didn't need that from him, either.

He watched her as she buckled Grace up, then returned to the house presumably to get Jennifer without a single glance his way. And why should she? She didn't want him around.

He wished he knew what had happened between that night of the book club meeting and now.

Regardless, Mia had made it fairly clear with her absence, her silence and now her pronouncement what she wanted.

He tightened his grip on Nola's halter rope, her colt ambling along behind her.

Then the door of the house opened and Nico came out first, Josh behind him and Mia, carrying Jennifer after him. Nate watched for a few moments, drawn to the kids, to Mia, wishing he could at least say goodbye.

He shook the feeling off. Clean break. That was best.

A gust of wind caught at the gate he had closed but not latched shut and as it screeched open, the colt kicked up its heels and bolted toward the unexpected freedom.

And everything happened at once.

Nola pulled at the halter rope, her eyes rolling as she tried to keep her attention on her colt. She reared and Nate saw Nico pull free from Mia's hand, arms out as if to stop the colt as he ran across the yard.

"Nico, stay with your mother!" Nate yelled, trying to control his frantic mare.

The colt and Nico were on a collision course and Nola was going nuts.

Just then Nola gave one hard jerk and broke free.

She trumpeted her fear and started toward her colt just as the gate slammed shut again.

The colt ran against the gate and whinnied, the harsh clang and the noise catching Nico's attention.

Nate didn't know what to do first. His frantic gaze shot around the corral and he saw a rope hanging from one of the posts. He caught it, then vaulted over the fence, praying Nola would stay in the corral while he caught the colt.

He swung the rope while he ran, part of his attention on Nico and the colt that was jumping around and the other part of his attention on Nola, who was screaming from the corral.

Nate swung a loop over his head, praying as he released it. The noose sailed through the air and then, thank the Lord, landed precisely over the colt's head.

He tugged at the colt and managed to drag it back to the corral, but as soon as he opened the gate to let the colt inside, Nola reared, her front feet windmilling.

And she burst free.

Nate watched in horror as Nola ran past him, her eyes wild, not seeing her colt trailing behind Nate.

She was headed directly toward Nico.

"Nate, don't go," he heard Nico call out.

Nate registered Nico's call on one level, but right now he had to save him. He tossed the rope aside, ran toward the boy, reaching for him, praying he would save him before the horse came at him.

"Nate, Nate!" Nico called out just as Nate managed to catch him, roll and move him out of the way of the crazed mare. "I don't want you to go."

Astonishment at what he had just heard distracted Nate for a split second. He pulled back, staring at Nico, who was looking past him, pointing. "Watch out!" he yelled.

Nate turned in time to see Nola spin again, then her rear hoof flashed out. He felt a sudden jolt, a flash of lightning-sharp pain.

And then everything went black.

Move. Go help him.

Mia could only stare, frozen with helpless fear as she saw Nate's head snap back. Then he crumpled to the ground still holding Nico. She shook off her fear, running toward Nate, her own maternal instinct kicking in. She waved her arms and yelled at Nola who, by now, had settled down.

The horse shook her head once as if to establish that she was still in charge, then trotted off to the open corral gate to rejoin her colt that, thankfully, had stayed in the corral.

"Josh, make sure to close the gate," Mia called out as she dropped to the ground beside Nate and Nico.

Nate lay still as a corpse, his arms wrapped around Nico, his body still protecting him.

"Mom, help," Nico called out as he tried to wriggle free.

Mia's heart tightened. Nico was talking. But she couldn't rejoice in the moment. Not with Nate lying on the ground, blood dripping from the gash in his forehead onto his jacket—his lucky jacket—his face pale as paper. Her thoughts whirled as she tried to process what to do first.

Call 911.

Stop the bleeding.

She got up, shooting a quick glance behind her. Josh

was methodically latching the gate, both horses were inside. She ran to the car, grabbed her phone and diaper bag, punching in the numbers as she hurried back to Nate's side.

"Are you okay?" she asked Nico as she yanked a cloth out of the diaper bag, sandwiching the phone between her shoulder and ear.

Nico nodded, his wide eyes fixed on Nate. Mia wanted to ask him more, to hear him speak again, but the operator was on the line.

She rattled off what she had seen, then had to repeat it. She followed the operator's instructions while her heart seesawed between panic, fear and a curious elation at hearing her son finally speaking.

But for now her attention was on Nate lying on the ground at her knees while she kept pressure on the ugly wound on his head.

His eyelids fluttered and for a hopeful moment she thought they might open. But they never did. His head still lolled to one side, blood from the gash seeping onto the cloth Jennifer had, only moments ago, been clutching to her cheek.

Mia, following the instructions of the operator, resisted the urge to move him, to try to make him more comfortable.

"The ambulance will be there in less than ten minutes," the calm voice on the other end of the line assured her, talking to her and to the drivers of the ambulance. "Just keep applying pressure."

All Mia could do was follow her instructions and pray. Pray for her son, crouching silently opposite her, holding Nate's hand, and pray for the man who had slowly insinuated himself into her life and heart.

"Let Your will be done," Mia prayed, once again far too aware of how helpless she truly was and how little control she had over her life.

And her heart.

"Is he going to be okay?" she heard Josh ask.

Mia gave him a quick smile for an answer, then the operator was asking her another question. She heard whimpering coming from the van and sent Josh there to keep his sisters entertained.

Nico stayed where he was, holding Nate's hand like a lifeline.

A few minutes and what seemed like a lifetime later, she heard the ominous wail of the ambulance as it drew closer and finally came onto the yard.

Nico's eyes grew wide with fear as the paramedics rushed over and Mia's busy mind spared a moment to wonder how this was going to affect him now.

One paramedic gently pulled Mia aside and another tried to take Nico. He fought her, reaching out to Nate.

"No. Nate, please don't go," he called out.

The sound of his panicked voice raised a storm of emotions that Mia couldn't sort out. Exhilaration, concern, relief and fear.

She pushed down her increasing panic, clinging to her steady prayer.

"Please, Lord, keep Nate safe."

As the paramedics strapped Nate to a board, Mia took Nico and held him close. She murmured encouragement to him as they watched Nate being moved to a stretcher then wheeled toward the ambulance and trundled inside. Then, as she had the first day she met

Nate, she heard the wail of sirens as the ambulance left the yard.

And her prayers increased.

Chapter Fifteen

"Poor Nate," Josh said, folding his hands over his chest as Mia tucked him in bed. "We have to pray for him, don't we?"

"Yes, we do. That was hard to see, wasn't it?" Mia could still hear the smack of Nola's hoof connecting with Nate, the way Nate's head snapped back then thudded lifelessly to the ground, blood streaming from his head.

After the ambulance left, Mia called Denny and Evangeline and they had immediately gone to the hospital, leaving Ella with Renee in town.

An hour ago they had called to say that Nate was conscious and in deep pain. He had suffered a concussion and would be kept overnight for observation. Denny joked how it was lucky Nate was kicked in the head. Anywhere else and he might have sustained some real damage.

But the humor was lost on Mia.

"Are you sure he's okay?" Josh asked, the worry in his voice mirroring her own.

"Uncle Denny said he is, so we have to believe that," Mia replied, gently stroking his hair back from his face.

Nico climbed onto the bed beside Josh and slumped down, the picture of abject misery. "I want Nate," he said quietly, as if he was still getting used to his voice.

Mia's heart was torn. Hearing her son talk was the one bright and shining spot in all the hard things that had happened the past few days.

"I know, honey," she said, stroking Nico's face, then pulling him onto her lap.

"I hope Nate's heart is okay," Josh continued, tapping his folded hands on his chest. He yawned and rubbed his eyes, then eased out a sigh.

"What do you mean, his heart is okay?" Mia asked. As far as Denny and Evangeline had heard, Nate's heart was just fine.

Josh looked back at her as if puzzled. "Nate said that if he opened his heart it would hurt. And you said the horse kick opened his heart."

Mia stared at her son, trying to understand what he was saying. "I said that the kick opened up a gash in his head, is that what you're talking about?"

Now it was Josh's turn to look puzzled. Then he shook his head. "Nate said that he was afraid to open his heart. That it would hurt if he did. And that he said he didn't know what he would do if you pushed him away." Josh shot his mother a puzzled frown. "But you didn't push Nate. The horse kicked him."

His comments and questions came at her like disparate statements she struggled to piece together.

"When did Nate say this?" she asked.

"When we were building birdhouses," Josh continued. "He said it to Denny. He sounded really sad."

The same afternoon she had overheard Nate saying that he had to leave.

What had he meant? She looked down at Josh, knowing she wouldn't get the full story from him, but she knew there was someone who could tell her.

"I'm sure Nate's heart is good," Mia assured him, then bent over to kiss him good-night.

She prayed with the boys, adding her own prayer for answers and wisdom.

She checked on her sleeping daughters, then walked downstairs, made a pot of coffee, pulled out her Bible and sat and read while she waited for Denny and Evangeline to return and update her on Nate's progress.

Half an hour later, the sound of the outside door and the subdued sounds of Denny and Evangeline's voices on the porch combined to weave a web of dread around Mia.

She closed her Bible, her hands clutching the fresh cup of coffee she had just poured for herself. When they came into the kitchen and she saw the anxiety on their faces, the web tightened.

"So. How is he? Is he going to be okay?" The words spilled out in a rush of worry and fear.

Denny gave her a careful smile as he shifted Ella to Evangeline. "He has about a dozen stitches in his head, but yes, he'll be fine. Like I told you, the doctors simply want to keep him in for observation. He'll be discharged tomorrow."

"What did you think, Evangeline?" Mia needed a second opinion.

"I think he'll be okay." She laid her hand on Mia's shoulder and squeezed lightly. "Just give me a minute to put Ella to bed and I'll join you."

Evangeline left and Denny poured himself a cup of coffee and sat down with Mia.

He gave her a reassuring, fatherly pat on the arm. "He'll be okay, you know. He's tough. He's lived through a lot worse."

"I'm guessing you're talking about Karl?" Mia asked.

Denny nodded as he spooned some sugar into his mug. He stirred it, the faint clinking of his spoon the only sound in the quiet of the kitchen. Then Denny leaned back and gave her a penetrating look.

"Nate's talking about leaving when he gets out of the hospital," Denny said, pausing to take a sip of coffee. "Stop me if I'm sticking my nose in where I shouldn't, but can you tell me why? He said it was what you wanted."

Mia frowned, puzzled that Denny would draw that conclusion. "He was the one who was talking about leaving."

Now it was Denny's turn to look confused. "Do you mean for the futurity?"

"No. I mean for good."

Denny shook his head. "Nate never said anything about leaving permanently. In fact, he had been making plans to stay."

"Stay? Where?"

"Here. He had been looking at the Miedema place. Looking to buy it."

His words fell into her mind like pebbles, each one creating ripples that intersected, disturbing her perceptions.

"Buy it? But…I thought he was leaving."

"For the futurity, yes. But then he was coming back."

"But I heard…I heard him say that he had to do what he had to do. That he had to leave."

Denny looked taken aback. "When did you hear that?"

Mia tried to not blush. She hadn't deliberately eavesdropped when she overheard this. She had been on her way to deliver Nate's jacket.

The jacket with the phone number of Lacy Miedema in the pocket.

"Can I ask you something personal about Nate?" Mia asked, suspecting that what Josh had said and what she had overheard were part of the same conversation.

"Ask and I'll see if I can answer it," Denny replied.

Mia hesitated a moment, not sure how to word the question that had been hovering at the edge of her mind ever since she came down from her son's bedroom.

"This evening, when I was tucking Josh in, he asked about Nate's heart." Mia suppressed a faint blush but then forged on. "He told me he had heard Nate say something about being afraid of opening his heart. That it would hurt if I pushed him away. Can you tell me what he meant by that?"

Denny didn't answer right away, which made Mia wonder if she had overstepped a boundary. Then he leaned forward, looking into his coffee as if looking for inspiration there.

"Nate has had a tough life," he said. "I'm sure he's told you a few things."

"He told me about Karl."

"Did he tell you how he ended up with Karl?"

Mia shook her head. She remembered wondering but the conversation had moved on and she never thought to ask the question about his mother.

"Nate was about seven when his mother moved in with Karl. She was a single mother who had drifted from place to place. She would live with a guy, leave Nate with him for a couple of days at a time, then come back. Then she met Karl. He had a ranch and was well-off, so she moved in with him. She settled down, but after a couple of years, Karl's true colors came through. She decided she didn't want any part of that and left. But she left Nate behind. She abandoned him. That haunted Nate for years."

Mia felt her breath catch in her throat as she listened to the painful story of Nate's childhood.

"When he came to live with us he was wary, careful and never said anything about his past," Denny said. "Living with our family was like an out of control rodeo and I'm sure it was a huge switch. But in time he grew less reserved and slowly opened up. That's when I found out about how he felt when his mother left. Abandoned. Afraid and very cautious about, as Josh had said, opening his heart to anyone. I know when my parents died, it was another blow that made him retreat emotionally again."

Then Denny looked over at Mia. "And then he came here and he met you."

Mia sat back in her chair, feeling the gentle force of Denny's words.

"What do you mean?" she whispered, part of her knowing exactly what he was implying.

"He met you and he realized that he had found what he had been looking for. An independent woman who he respected, cared for. A woman who loved her children without reservation. A woman he could see building a life with."

Mia stared at him, her hopeful heart quivering at what he said.

"And what Josh had overheard was Nate telling me that he was afraid of his growing feelings for you and for your children," Denny continued. "He couldn't believe that something good could happen to him. That's why he needed time to think about all this. But he always had plans to come back to you."

More questions circled.

But she knew that anything else she needed to find out, she had to find out from Nate.

"Thanks for this," she said to Denny, getting up and setting her coffee cup in the sink. "Thanks for what you told me."

"I hope it helped," he said.

"It did," she replied, her voice full of conviction and her heart laced with hope. "It helped a lot."

Nate heard a rustling in the hospital room but kept his eyes closed. The pain medication he had just received hadn't kicked in yet and his head felt as if a sledgehammer had split his skull open. Every time he opened his eyes, he felt the hit again. Though he was glad he was going back to Denny and Evangeline's place to recuperate, Mia was there. And he wasn't sure how he was going to deal with seeing her again.

Denny had brought him a clean shirt and pants last night and he had changed into them this afternoon. He was resting on the bed, waiting for the doctor to come and discharge him.

But he wasn't in any mood to talk to anyone. So he turned his head to the side, a silent directive to any nurse to leave him alone.

He heard the scrape of a chair that cut into his head and then, as whoever had come into the room settled into the chair beside him, he heard a faint sniff and caught the scent of lilacs.

Mia?

He turned his head too quickly and pain knifed through his skull. A groan escaped as he opened his eyes.

And there she was, sitting on the chair beside him.

He couldn't stop the lift of his heart. The expectation that quickened his breath.

Her dark eyes showed her concern as did the faint lines bracketing her mouth, and he tamped down his reactions. She was only here because she was a caring, loving person and she felt sorry for him.

"Hey, there," she whispered as a careful smile teased at her mouth. "I'd ask how you're doing, but I think the bandages and bruises say it all."

Nate attempted a smile but at the same time he flashed back to their last conversation. How she had asked him to leave and pushed him away.

"I'm okay," he said, keeping his tone noncommittal. Then a memory assailed him. "How is Nico? Did I really hear him calling out my name?"

Mia's smile shone. "Yes. I'm bringing him to see Dr. Schuler on Monday. He's been speaking more since yesterday."

"I wonder what triggered it."

"I think it was his fear of you leaving."

Nate wasn't sure what to say to that. Nico's connection to him was still a puzzle. "I'm glad he's talking again. That must ease a huge burden for you."

She nodded, the hopeful look on her face creating

possibilities. "So what brings you here?" he asked, trying to keep his tone brusque. Trying to maintain some distance between them.

Mia's hesitant smile faded, but then she did a surprising thing. She reached over and swept his hair back from his bandages. Her fingers brushed his forehead, cool, soft and inviting.

Nate pushed back his reaction. He had to stay focused. He couldn't allow himself to get drawn into renegade emotions. He had to keep himself aloof from her.

But even as one part of his mind tried to convince himself of this, he couldn't stifle the hope her presence had awakened.

"I came for a couple of reasons," Mia said, her hand slipping back to her lap. "One was to apologize for what I said yesterday. About how I thought you should leave. I…I was laboring under a misapprehension."

"Been reading Dickens, have we?" he joked, hoping to deflect with humor.

"No, but I have been talking to Denny," she said, seeming to ignore his joke. "I've found out things I didn't know. Found out that I was wrong about you and that I was wrong to push you away." She brushed her hand over her head, pushing her short hair away from her face. It immediately fell back, framing her thick-lashed eyes. A flush heightened the color of her cheeks, and as she looked at him he sensed a shift in the atmosphere. A return to the awareness that had once arced between them.

He tried to fight it, but found himself slowly drawn back to her.

"What makes you say that?" Nate prompted, not sure

if the knock to his head was making him delusional or if she was backtracking from what she had said yesterday.

Or maybe she just felt sorry for him.

"I found out about your visit to the Miedema place," she continued. "With Lacy."

He frowned, then winced as pain stabbed behind his eyeballs. "Sorry," he said, "I don't know where you're going with this."

Then, to his surprise, she took his hand in hers. "Do you have time to listen to me?"

"I'm not allowed to leave the hospital until tonight, so yeah, I got time."

Mia's laugh ignited a faint spark of hope. Then her expression grew serious.

"I don't know exactly where to start," she said, gently running her hand over his. "I feel foolish but I need to tell you how things looked for me. Why I said you should leave." She paused, her eyes lowered, watching her hand as it traced the scars on the back of his hand. Some of which came from working with his horses.

Some from Karl.

But he kept quiet, letting the silence hang between them, rife with expectancy.

"I know what I am. A mother of four children. I know that it would take a special person to be…be with me. When I saw you with Lacy Miedema, when I found her phone number in the pocket of your coat, it was as if all my doubts had found an outlet."

Lacy? Why was she talking about Lacy? "What? What are you talking about?"

Mia gave him a patient smile. "I thought you were attracted to her. I thought I didn't matter to you any-more, and why would I? She's attractive—"

"You're a beautiful woman, Mia. An amazing woman," Nate interrupted her as he tightened his grip on her hand, slowly beginning to understand what had happened. "How could you think that I'd be interested in Lacy?"

"I found her phone number in the pocket of your coat. And then, at book club, she and you went outside."

"Yeah. To see Tango and to talk about her dad's place. I was thinking of buying it."

"I know that now, but you have to understand how it looked to me. I saw you with her—young, pretty, single, unattached—and compared her to me. Older, divorced, messy, tangled life and four children. I couldn't imagine how you could choose me over her."

"But I was never interested in her." Nate felt a slow realization dawn on him. "You were jealous of her?"

Mia gave a tight nod.

"You didn't need to be." He drew in a quick breath, but the pain that had sliced through his head was now reduced to a dull throb. The pain medication must have kicked in. "I was never interested in her."

She looked up at him and in spite of his assurances he still saw doubt on her face.

"You don't believe me, do you?"

"I want to," she said quietly. Then she sighed. "I have my reasons why I don't."

"Tell me," he encouraged.

Mia bit her lip as if hesitating, then started talking. "I told you that Al left me when I was expecting. But I didn't tell you the other reason. I found out later that he was cheating on me. With a much younger, thinner and prettier girl."

"Al was an idiot," Nate said, his voice growing harsh. "Don't judge yourself by his actions."

Mia's smile grew at his words and in spite of his desire to protect his own heart, he knew he had to let her know his feelings. Needed to assure her of how important she was to him.

"You know I was attracted to you the first time I saw you."

"And then you found out I had kids."

Nate was quiet a moment, trying to find the right words to express his initial reaction to her. "It wasn't the kids. I love kids. It was the fact that, as a mother, you would need someone I didn't think I could be. You needed someone who could commit to sticking around. I didn't dare make that commitment until…until I got to know you. Got to love you."

Mia stared at him as if she hadn't heard him properly. "Love me?"

He squeezed her hand again, the only way he could assure her right now. Then he sat up, facing her directly. "Yes. Love you. I didn't think I could do that. Didn't dare to."

Mia smiled at that. "Josh was worried about you. Apparently, he heard you say that you were afraid of opening your heart and he thought that when you were injured that maybe your heart was hurt."

Nate released a light laugh. "I was afraid. That's why, when you said I should leave, I took you at your word. I thought for sure that you didn't want me around."

Mia shook her head. "No. I did want you around. I said that because of something I misheard. I didn't think you were coming back." She lifted his hand and brushed her lips over the back of it. "You mean more to me than any man ever has. And that made me afraid, too. I was guarding my heart, as well. I was just as afraid as you."

Nate hardly believed what she was saying. Could hardly believe that the relationship he thought was shattered beyond repair was slowly being mended and re-made.

"So you told me to leave," he said, his voice quiet, uncondemning.

Mia nodded, holding his gaze this time, her eyes steady. "I wanted to be the one in control this time around. I wanted to be the one who made the decisions. I thought it would be easier if I told you to leave than if you were the one who left me."

"But I wasn't leaving. I was only going to the futurity and then I was coming back."

"I know that now," she returned. "I talked to Denny. He told me that you were thinking of buying the Mi-edema place."

Nate was suddenly tired of the distance between them. He carefully got up, then he pulled Mia out of her chair and drew her close to him, reveling in the feel of her fragile form in his arms. "I am thinking of buying it. I want to make a home for you and for your kids. I want to be beside you, supporting you and being a partner to you."

Mia looked up at him, her hands now resting on his chest. And once again he saw the glimmer of tears in her eyes.

"I know you've lost so much the past while," he said. "But I want to help you rebuild and be there for you."

She could only shake her head, looking at him. "Is this true? Is this real?"

"Maybe this will convince you," he said as he drew

her close and caught her lips in a kiss. "I love you, Mia," he said against her mouth, brushing his lips over her cheeks, her eyes, her forehead, ignoring the dull throb of pain in his own. "I love your kids and I want to make a life with you."

"I love you, too," she whispered, gently touching his face. "So much."

She kissed him again and as they drew back, Nate felt as if all the loose ends of his life had finally been woven into a whole.

"As soon as I get discharged, I want to go to the ranch. Tell the kids." Then he smiled. "Talk to Nico. Make plans for our future," he said, brushing his fingers over her beloved face. "A future together."

"Together. I like the sound of that."

As he kissed her again he knew he had found what he'd been seeking all his life. Family. Home. Love.

Epilogue

"Too bad about second place," Arden said, clapping Nate on the shoulder as they walked out of the arena, Tango following behind. "I think your horse would have placed first if he had a better group of cows to work with."

"I'm happy enough with second," Nate said, leading Tango through the fenced-off alley to the pens behind the arena, thankful it was over. "All things considered, Tango did his best and that's what matters."

The competition was over. The crowd was still cheering the first-place winner, who was now cantering his horse around the arena in his victory lap.

"He's got some great lines, good control. I'd like to talk to you about stud fees."

Nate gave him a quick look and nodded, and Arden looked like he was about to say more when Nate heard voices calling his name.

"Looks like you got your own fan club," Arden said with a laugh as Nico and Josh ran toward him, Mia behind carrying Grace, Denny with Jennifer and Evangeline holding Ella.

"We saw you ride," Josh called out, grabbing Nate's hand.

"I saw you, too," Nico repeated as Nate bent down and swung him up, then set him on Tango's back.

"You did great," Mia said, flinging an arm around his neck. He took a moment and dropped a kiss on her lips, giving her a happy smile. "And so did you, Tango," she added, taking a moment to pat him, as well.

Grace reached out for him and Nate caught her in his arms and gave her a tight hug. She laughed and grabbed for his cowboy hat.

"You can't have that, Grace," Nico complained. "It's Nate's."

But Nate just grinned and dropped his hat on her head.

His heart swelled with joy and pride. That all of them had come down to the competition to watch him meant more than he could ever tell them.

"So, I don't imagine you'll be coming to my ranch tomorrow to work for me," he heard Arden saying.

Nate shook his head. "No. I've got other priorities."

"Quite a few of them, I can see," Arden replied.

"Nothing I can't handle," Nate returned, giving Mia a quick smile and a wink.

"Well, I'll let you get back to your family," Arden said.

Nate looked over the gathered group and felt a settling in his soul.

His family.

He liked the sound of that.

"So, should we go home?" Mia asked.

And Nate liked the sound of that even better.

He gave Mia another kiss, shifted Grace in his arms

and with everyone gathered around, they walked out of the arena to the vehicles.

Next stop Hartley Creek. And home.

* * * * *

Dear Reader:

Both Mia and Nate had issues from their past that they had to let go of in order to move forward. Nate had to learn to release his need to prove himself to a man who was dead, and Mia had to release herself from her ex-husband's perception of herself. Many times we let the past define our present. Thankfully, our Lord not only deals with us where we are today, He helps us put away the guilt and the hurt of the past, giving us hope for a renewed future. I pray that if you are dealing with scars of the past that you can see yourself as a new creation in Christ.

Blessings,

Carolyne Aarsen

P.S. I love to hear from my readers. Write me at caarsen@xplornet.com or stop by my website at www.carolyneaarsen.com and sign up for my newsletter to keep up with news and upcoming releases.

Questions for Discussion

1. Nate seems taken aback when he finds out Mia has four children. Why do you think he reacts that way?

2. Even though Nate says he's not a kid person, he is very good with Mia's children. Why do you think Nate downplays his talent with children?

3. When Mia's business burns down, she loses everything. Have you ever gone through a similar experience? How did you cope?

4. One of Mia's sons, Nico, stops speaking after the fire. Why do you think he does this?

5. Mia believes she already had her chance at love, and doesn't expect another. Do you agree with her? Do you think each of us only gets one shot at love, or do we get many chances?

6. Nate suffered abuse at the hands of his stepfather. How did this affect him in his adult life?

7. Why do you think Nate has such a hard time accepting the money his stepfather willed to him? What would you have done in the same situation?

8. Mia loves her children and would do anything for them. Was she right in being so overprotective of them? Why or why not?

9. When Nate is injured by the horse, Mia realizes that she cares for him very much. Have you ever come to understand something clearer after an emergency or tragedy? Discuss.

10. What are some of the things Mia and Nate will have to deal with in their future?

REQUEST YOUR FREE BOOKS!

2 FREE INSPIRATIONAL NOVELS
PLUS 2
FREE
MYSTERY GIFTS

Love Inspired®

LI13R

SPECIAL EXCERPT FROM

*Widowed mom Suzie Kent is desperate to help her
troubled son. Is her only hope the man she blames for her
husband's death?*

*Read on for a preview of
HER UNLIKELY COWBOY by Debra Clopton,
Book #3 in the SUNRISE RANCH series.*

"Suzie Kent. It's good to see you." Tucker McDermott's
eyes crinkled around the edges, but concern stamped his
expression, as if he knew the dismay shooting through her.

Her breath had flown from her lungs and she had no
words as she looked into the face of the man she held responsible for her husband's death.

The man she was also counting on to help her save her son.

The man she wasn't prepared to see, though she'd just
driven three hours with a moving van and plans to live on
Sunrise Ranch, the ranch his family owned and operated.

Her world tilted as she realized whose clean, tangy
aftershave was teasing her senses and whose unbelievably
intense gaze had her insides suddenly rioting. His hair was
jet-black and his skin deeply tanned, making his deep blue
eyes startling in their intensity.

"Tucker," she managed, hoping her voice didn't wobble.

Moving to Dew Drop, Texas, to Tucker's family's Sunrise
Ranch, asking for his help, had taken everything she had
left emotionally—and that hadn't been much, since her
husband had given his life in the line of duty for fellow
marine Tucker two years earlier.

Tucker grimaced, trying to keep most of his weight off Suzie and Abe, but his hip clearly hurt.

"Thank y'all for helping me," he said, his gaze snagging on hers again and holding. "I've got it from here, though." He pulled one arm from around her and the other from around her son, Abe.

"Are you sure?" she asked, even though she wanted to step away from him in the worst way. "Do we need to get you to your vehicle?

Tucker limped a few painful steps away from them. "I'm okay," he said gruffly. "It'll just take a few minutes for the throbbing to go away." He glanced ruefully at the donkeys on the road. "What a mess. They act like they own the road."

Abe chuckled. "They sure took you out."

"By the way, I'm Tucker McDermott. I was a friend of your dad's and I owe him my life. He was an amazing man." Tucker cleared his throat. "I'm glad you've come to Dew Drop. And the boys of Sunrise Ranch are looking forward to meeting you."

Will this cowboy heal her family—and her heart?

Pick up HER UNLIKELY COWBOY to find out.
Available May 2014
wherever Love Inspired® Books are sold.

Grace parked in the shade across from the school and released her three-year-old from his booster seat and looked for her two children.

It wasn't hard to spot her eldest. His red hair stood out like a lit traffic flare at an accident scene when he left the main building and started in her direction. Then he paused, pivoted and ran right up to a total stranger.

The man crouched to embrace the boy, setting Grace's nerves on edge and causing her to react immediately.

"Hey! What do you think you're doing?"

The figure stood in response to her challenge. The brim of a cap and dark glasses masked his eyes, yet there was something very familiar about the way he moved.

Grace gaped. It couldn't be. But it was. "Dylan?"

He placed a finger against his lips. "Shush. Not here. We need to talk."

When he removed the glasses, Grace was startled to glimpse an unusual gleam in her estranged husband's eyes, as if he might be holding back tears—which, of course, was out of the question, knowing him.

"If you want to speak to me you can do it through my lawyer, the way we agreed."

"This has nothing to do with our divorce. It's much more important than that."

Grace's first reaction was disappointment, followed rapidly by resentment. "What can possibly be more important than our marriage and the future of our children?"

"I'm beginning to realize that my priorities need adjustment, but that's not why we have to talk. In private."

"What could you possibly have to say to me that can't be said right here?"

"Let me put it this way, Grace," Dylan said quietly, cupping her elbow and leaning closer. "You can either come with me and listen to what I have to say, or get ready to save a bunch of money, because you won't have to pay your divorce attorney."

"Why on earth not?"

Dylan scanned the crowd and clenched his jaw before he said, "Because you'll probably be a widow."

*Will Grace and Dylan find a way to save
their marriage and their lives?
Pick up FAMILY IN HIDING to find out.
Available May 2014 wherever
Love Inspired® Suspense books are sold.*